To: Elaine

Summer

of Stars

The Past Lives of Lola Ray Book One

Thanks for
supporting my
work! Enjoy!

Leslee Horner

Leslee
Horner
2014

Summer of Stars

The Past Lives of Lola Ray Book One

To my husband, Mark, for loving and supporting me on this journey.

Acknowledgements

First and foremost, I must give a huge thanks to the Wednesday Night Writers (Adrian, Leigh, Gina, Noanne, and Linda) whose guidance and insight helped this book come to life. Thanks to Leigh Muller and Adrian Fogelin for reading and critiquing the earliest draft and to Linda Sturgeon and Renee Liss for your input on the later draft. To Heather Whitaker and Gina Edwards, thank you for your editing expertise that made it possible to put this novel out into the world. I am ever grateful to Glenn Miller for creating a beautiful cover and website.

I've had so many readers and cheerleaders along the way, but I must give special thanks to the teen readers—Lauren Sumners, Madison Hecker, Jessica Hecker, Hartley Denmark, Cynthia Myers, and Dominique Akinyemi—who took the time to read SUMMER OF STARS at its various stages and share their thoughts. Knowing that my target audience enjoyed the book made the process of publishing that much easier to undertake!

I especially give thanks to my family. My husband, Mark, and daughters, Bella and Callee, have been ever patient and supportive of me over these years that I've blazed down this author trail. They've graciously accepted sharing Mom with Lola and Ian. To Heather Wilson and Kristin Benesowitz, my sisters in spirit, I thank you for cheering me on, listening to me talk about my dreams, and for reading my writing! I thank my parents, Brenda and Doug Simpson, for instilling in me a sense of patience and work ethic, both of which have carried me far on my path.

Finally, I want to honor my dear friend, Amy Stephens Pardue, who isn't here to see my book, but was one of my biggest champions. She called me a writer before I did.

Chapter 1

A piercing whistle alerts us that a train is approaching. As the noise grows louder, I have the urge to slam my gloved hands over my ears like a five-year-old. I'm not five though. I'm fifteen and about as terrified as I've ever been. The whistle stops and I hear boots hit the gravel as soldiers march between the train tracks and the crowd. I stare at the swastikas on their uniforms while mindlessly tracing the yellow Star of David on my heavy wool coat. I stand in a circle with my mother and my father, our three small suitcases on the ground between us. They came for us in the dark before dawn, told us to bring one bag each, and led us miles to this train station. I scan the faces of the others around us. Their noses and cheeks are red from the cold, their eyes are anxious. Mother twists a handkerchief around her thumb then raises her hands to her face and breathes into them.

"We're going to be all right, Love," Papa says, leaning down and kissing the top of her head.

She smiles and a tear slips down her cheek. She reaches out and squeezes my hand. As I cling to my mother, I am aware of the cries of children. In the crowd, there are dozens. I spot one small boy standing at his father's side, crying and shivering. The boy reaches out like a beggar. My gaze follows his outstretched hand and I see a young Nazi soldier. He can't be much older than me. His eyes are anxious, conflicted. He looks around, checking that no one is watching before he moves toward the child. He reaches into his pocket and retrieves a small foil-wrapped candy, which he quickly places in the boy's hand. The child's face lights up as he surveys the treasure. I look back at the soldier just in time to glimpse the hint of a smile vanish from his face.

The train pulls into the station, brakes squealing. I take a deep breath, brisk air on the inhale, and look to the sky. The day is grey. My fingers and toes are numb from being in the cold for so long. We've dreaded this day but knew we'd find ourselves here eventually. Our family business, Frankl's Dressmakers, was destroyed months ago when our village was raided. Since then we've shared a home, under close watch by the Gestapo, with five other Jewish families.

There has been a great deal of talk and speculation about the camps. Most of it bad, a little good. I don't know what I believe. I only know the sick feeling in the pit of my stomach suggests something unimaginable. I should be in school right now, sitting next to my best friend, Sarah, and trying not to giggle during lessons. But Sarah was taken away weeks ago and now I'm here, staring at the wheels of the train cars, watching them roll to a stop. The silence among my people, the Jews waiting to board this train, lifts as muffled conversations erupt. The whispered exchanges bring to mind a hive of buzzing bees. Their commotion could be mistaken for excitement except I know that it is really confusion at best, terror at worst.

Where will we find ourselves at the end of this journey?

I jerked awake, the library copy of *The Diary of Anne Frank* slipped off my chest and landed with a thud on the floor beside my bed. I grabbed the clock. It wasn't even midnight yet. It was still June twentieth and I was still fourteen-years-old, lying in bed, in the home I shared with my mom and dad on a quiet suburban street. I was Lola Elena Ray, not that scared girl waiting for a train in the cold. Who was she? Where *were* they taking her? A breeze swept through the room. I'd forgotten to close the window.

I slammed the snooze button on my alarm clock, but the noise didn't stop. Waking up at eight in the morning on a summer day was entirely inappropriate, especially on my birthday. I flung the covers back and shuffled to the window to see what the noise was. A U-Haul was backing into the driveway across the street. I crawled back into bed and pulled the quilt over my head. The shivering little boy and anxious-eyed young soldier flashed through my mind. Last night's dream was entirely too real—like I'd actually been there. I felt a sense of dread wondering where the train would have taken me.

I got up. The extra sleep wasn't worth it if it meant I might fall back into that dream. I carefully made the bed, ignoring the knots in my stomach. One thing could calm my nerves, but I'd promised myself that when I turned fifteen, I would try to be more normal. I couldn't control the anxious thoughts that popped into my head, but maybe I could resist the urge to vacuum. I sat on the bed surveying the perfect carpet lines I'd made the night before. Everyone's a little OCD, right?

I breathed deeply into what Mom's therapist calls my heart space and thought of a positive memory: my eleventh birthday in Panama City Beach, floating in the clear Gulf of Mexico water with Mom and Dad. Mom taught me this relaxation technique before end of course tests last month when I was a complete ball of stress. I'd taken to doing the exercise often and couldn't ignore the theme in the memories I conjured. Calm.

I walked out of my bedroom just as Mom was coming up the

stairs, carrying a stack of folded laundry.

"I'm going to pick up a housewarming gift for the new neighbors," she said. "You want to come?"

She passed the clothes to me. Her eyes darted from me to the clothes then to her watch. She seemed wired, like she'd had way too much coffee. It was also odd that she was dressed and wearing makeup at this hour of the morning. Something was off.

"Isn't it a little early?" I asked.

"They're moving in right now. I was thinking of taking them brunch." She tucked her long blonde hair behind her ears and surveyed my pajamas. "I can wait for you to get ready if you want to come."

"That's okay. You go without me."

"Okay." She smiled and went back down the steps. I stayed at the top, giving her time to realize what she'd failed to say. When I heard the garage door go up, I knew it was a lost cause. My mom had forgotten my birthday. The knots were back.

I walked into the bathroom and closed the door behind me. Running the brush through my long, mousy, brown hair, I looked down only to notice the way my shirt fit too tightly across my stomach. I pressed my hand against it and sucked in. In anticipation of my fifteenth year being the year I would finally feel like a normal teenager, I had tried out for the cheerleading squad. The Universe confirmed my plan when I actually made the team. Now I wondered if they made uniforms in size twelve.

Before heading downstairs, I crept into Dad's office to get my laptop. I wasn't surprised to find him on the couch, snoring loudly. For the past few weeks, his work had picked up and the time he spent in his home office was starting to extend into the wee hours of the morning. I walked carefully past the couch, noticing the bald spot on the back of his head. It seemed the hair had just jumped off his head and replanted itself along the top of his back between his shoulders. And speaking of his back, it seemed to be wider than ever. I tried not to worry about his weight and health and the mere fact that he was getting older. But it wasn't easy.

I reached across the desk for my laptop. My elbow hit Dad's mousepad. The screen refreshed and before me was a Twitter page with Dad's name on it, not the name of his business. I stared at his last update.

@zanyZandria Goodnight Dear. . . . sweet dreams!

It was typed six hours ago, two in the morning. I reached for the mouse.

"Watcha doing?" His groggy yet concerned voice came from behind me. I quickly clicked on the X.

"Just getting my laptop."

"Can't start the morning without your fix now, can you?" He sat on the edge of the couch rubbing his eyes.

I got up with my laptop tucked under my arm. "Guess not." I walked toward the door wondering who @zanyZandria was.

"Happy birthday, Lola," Dad called from behind me.

I turned around. "Thanks." At least he remembered my birthday.

All the way downstairs, I analyzed the tweet. Dear, why did he call her dear? Had he ever called Mom *dear*? How long had he known this Zandria? What was going on with the two of them? Is she the reason for this secret Twitter account? Forcing the thoughts out of my head, I plopped on the couch and opened the computer. Staring back at me from my Facebook wall were five birthday messages, including one from my best friend.

Hannah Parker 2-4-6-8 who do we appreciate? Lola! Happy Birthday babe! Miss you!

When Hannah left to spend the summer with her dad a few weeks ago, I thought I'd go crazy at first, but it wasn't all that bad. Before she left, she was obsessing over not making the cheerleading squad. I don't think she imagined I would make it and she wouldn't. Hopefully, she'd get over it before she came back.

Lola Ray Thanks for the birthday wishes. We've got new neighbors moving in across the street and a vacation on the horizon, pretty interesting day so far!

I couldn't have cared less about the neighbors and was only slightly excited about the trip to DC. The only thing interesting— if that was even the right word—about the first waking hour of my birthday was that my mom had forgotten it and I discovered my dad had a secret life online.

Chapter 2

"Toodle-Loo!" Mom walked through the kitchen doorway, sunglasses on, lugging a couple of overflowing grocery bags. "There's a few more in the car. Can you get them for me?"

Mouth full of cereal, I rose from the breakfast table and walked out the door. "Geez, Mom, what are you doing with all of this?" I yelled into the kitchen.

"I'm making the neighbors a gift basket."

Shaking my head, I grabbed the laundry basket she'd bought and a bag from the backseat of the Escape. When I came back inside, I placed them on the floor beside her. Soon the bags were empty and the kitchen table was covered in supplies for her gift basket. Pushing them aside, I found my bowl of cereal and took it to the counter.

"Is your father up yet?" She bit her tongue in concentration as she weaved an oversized ribbon through the plastic of the basket. "Maybe I should go check on him.

"No, Mom, you don't need to do that." I thought about the Twitter page and the message I'd just seen. I certainly didn't want Mom to see it. "He was down here eating a little while ago. Must be back to work now."

"I'm worried about him." She got up and walked toward me, pushing my leg aside as she opened the drawer under the microwave. "He's always in that office. Hasn't slept in our bed in more than a week."

"He works late and doesn't want to bother you, I bet." The Twitter account flashed through my mind, followed by an uneasy feeling in my gut.

"I suppose we can just blame it on that darn new client." She shrugged. "We gotta eat, right?"

I hopped down from the counter and rinsed the bowl out in the sink. Noticing Mom's eyes glaze over with intense focus, I walked out of the room. No mention yet of my birthday and from the looks of it, the bags only contained household supplies for the neighbors, no gifts for me. Fifteen was not looking good.

I sat in my spot on the sectional and reached for the laptop. A car door slammed outside. I rose from the couch, strolled to the window and peered through the blinds. A green pickup truck was in the driveway across the street, its bed full of boxes. I'd just missed the owner as he or she stepped into the garage. I stared, anxious for them to reappear.

"It's your fifteenth birthday, not your eighty-fifth. Can't you find a better use of your time than spying on the neighbors?" Dad bounced down the steps, coffee mug in hand.

"I'm just trying to get a look at the newbies."

"You hoping for the quarterback?" Dad placed a hand on my shoulder and peered out the window too.

"Camden Collins drives a Mustang and I'm quite content with him staying wherever it is that he lives."

"I'm impressed, my dear Lola."

"Why? Because I'm not so shallow that my dream is to be friends with the star football player?"

"No, because you know who the quarterback is." Dad laughed, patted my head and walked into the kitchen. He glided by again seconds later, steam rising from the cup. I sat back down, abandoning my mission to get a glimpse of the new neighbors.

"Lola," Mom called. "I'll be done with this soon. You want to get ready and go with me across the street?"

I looked at my laptop screen. Nothing new there. Dare I go with my mother to meet the new neighbors? With the mood she was in, there was no telling how she'd act. What if she was too friendly? She'd already bought too much for that basket. Maybe I needed to go, just to keep her from embarrassing us.

"Sure, why not?" I put the computer on the coffee table and bounded up the stairs, feeling strangely excited.

On the way to the bathroom, I noticed the door to Dad's office was open so I crept in. I stepped behind him and peeked over his shoulder. "What's with the new Twitter account?"

Just like that, the screen vanished. "Good grief, Lola. Why don't you give somebody a warning?"

"Sorry." I sank into the middle of the plaid couch where the permanent indentation was. "I thought you only tweeted for the business?"

"Uhm . . . I set this one up to follow sports and politics."

"Make any new friends?" I asked.

He twirled around in his chair to face me. "Found a few people that aren't too bad." He scratched the stubble on his chin.

"Mom still hasn't wished me happy birthday and she's acting weird."

"Oh, Sweetie, I'm sorry." The springs in the couch squeaked when he sat down. "Your mother's just been a bit scattered lately. She hasn't forgotten."

"Is she still taking her meds?"

He shook his head. "You know, I couldn't even tell you."

"Because you've been scattered too?" I looked at the computer screen and then into my father's eyes.

"Not scattered, just busy." He went back to his desk. "Now if you'll excuse me, I need to get back to this."

The tension in the air was thick. I paused before leaving the room, but lost the nerve to ask him anything else. As I showered, I thought about his answer to my question. How could he not know if Mom was off her meds? He always stayed on her about sticking to the schedule. She definitely wasn't her normal, medicated self. Making a welcome basket for the new neighbors was a perfect example of that.

I walked downstairs to find Mom. "You're still working?"

"It has taken me forever to get this darn bow right." She looked up from the basket, which was overflowing with all kinds of stuff. "You look cute!" She smiled as she eyed the outfit I'd chosen, a halter sundress and my black ballerina shoes.

"I thought I'd look nice for the neighbors . . . and my birthday." I looked down at the floor.

Mom gasped. "I am so sorry. I just got caught up in this good deed of mine." She came over and put her arms around me. I reluctantly hugged her back.

"It's okay," I said.

"Grab the basket and I'll meet you at the door."

I headed for the front door, while Mom stayed behind rustling through the junk drawer.

"Nick, we're going to meet the new neighbors. You want to come?" Mom called up the stairs as she joined me.

"No thanks," Dad called back.

"Suit yourself," she mumbled and opened the door for me. I followed her across the street, the heavy laundry basket resting on my hip. Her long, flowing skirt was see-through in the sunlight, making the silhouette of her thin legs obvious even though it reached her ankles. If only I had my mom's hips and thighs I wouldn't have to worry about the cheerleading uniform.

When we reached the front door, she grabbed the basket from

me and rang the bell. A child's high-pitched squeal came from the other side.

"Just a minute." This voice was deep and strong.

Mom shifted from one foot to the other. Just as she was leaning to set the basket down, the door flew open and before us stood a nice-looking man, about the same age as Dad, with grey hair.

"This is for you!" Mom pushed the basket into the man and let out a huge sigh of relief, as if she was the one who carried it across the street.

"Thank you! Wow." He turned and put the basket down. "Was there some sign out there that I didn't know about, reading 'Single Dad In Need'?"

Mom put her hand on his shoulder and let out an over-dramatic laugh. "A lucky guess I suppose."

"Well, your guess is greatly appreciated." He stuck out a hand. "I'm Wayne and this is Sammy." He signaled to the little boy who stepped out from the hallway where he'd been taking in the scene.

Mom pulled her long, blonde hair over her left shoulder. Leaning toward Wayne, she reached for his hand. Her eyes met his. "I'm Christine and this is Lola. We live right across the street."

"Why don't you guys come in and sit down?" Wayne held out his hand, encouraging us to move to the other room.

Mom swiped a box out of the basket and led the way. I couldn't help but notice Wayne staring at her left hand. Mom wears her wedding ring on her right hand because Grandma Ray, who was in charge of getting their rings engraved and sized, ordered Mom's ring one size too big so it never fit her smaller left ring finger. They never got it resized out of fear the engraving would get ruined. Mom held that against Grandma until she died. She was convinced Grandma had done it out of spite because

Mom was marrying her only son.

"This place seems to be coming together nicely. When did you start moving in?" Opening the fridge as if she owned the place, Mom slid the box in.

"The boys and I got in last night with the first load. Set the beds up and spent the first night here sans TV and computers."

"Boys?" Mom joined me on the leather couch across from the recliner Wayne had perched in. Sammy pushed a big dump truck around the middle of the floor where a coffee table should have been.

"Yeah, my oldest son is sixteen."

"Oh, so he'll go to school with Lola and me. I'm the art teacher over at Washington."

"You might already know him then. Ian White? He's been at Washington for two years."

"The name's not ringing a bell." Mom shook her head and looked at me. "What about you Lola?"

I shook my head.

"Well, Ian's more of a techie and if he's not messing with computers, he's on his skateboard."

"He'll get along great with my husband then. For the techie part that is." Mom started playing with her wedding ring.

Wayne leaned back in his chair and folded his arms. "So you're married?"

"Oh, yes. My husband, Nick, is a web designer who is lucky enough to get to work from home."

"That sounds great. My wife and I divorced because our work hours were so different, we rarely had face time."

Mom looked at him with pity. "I'm so sorry."

He shrugged. "It's okay, we're better like this. And now I'm thrilled to be in a quiet neighborhood instead of a noisy apartment complex."

"Your moving in is one of several reasons to celebrate. Let's have some cheesecake." Mom walked into the kitchen again and opened the fridge. "Where are the knives, Wayne?"

Wayne joined her. I could see Mom squeeze by him, gently placing one hand on his back as she did. Then she turned and whispered in his ear. Was she flirting? I felt my face grow hot. Why did she have to act like this? Was she this desperate for attention since Dad was so engrossed in Twitter? More drawers opened and closed, and then Wayne emerged holding a slice of cheesecake with a candle in it. Mom followed behind him with two more plates and belted out, "Happy birthday to you, happy birthday to you, happy birthday, dear Lola, happy birthday to you."

I forced a smile and blew out the candle. I happened to look up as the candle went out and saw him, Wayne's sixteen-year-old son Ian.

"Whose birthday?" He said as he tossed his keys and fedora onto the kitchen table. He was tall and thin, with light eyes and dark, almost black hair. He wore a white t-shirt and skinny jeans. My stomach flipped. He looked familiar to me, but not from school. I was almost positive I'd never seen him at school.

"Oh, great timing, son." Wayne put his hand on Ian's back and led him toward me. In my opinion, his timing couldn't have been worse. "This is Lola and Christine, our new neighbors. Lola goes to Washington."

"You're going to be a sophomore, right?"

I nodded, while praying the embarrassment I felt wasn't written all over my face.

"I've seen you around."

"You look familiar, too." I pulled the candle out of my slice of cake.

Mom pushed a plate into Ian's hands. "Celebrate with us."

He accepted the plate. "I'll have to take this with me. I've got some more unpacking to do." He looked at me and smiled before he left the room. "Happy birthday."

"Thanks." I looked down at my plate and thought of the excited feeling I'd gotten before coming here. It's like I knew without knowing that this boy was across the street.

Chapter 3

"Why did you do that?" I asked Mom as we walked back across the street. "Didn't you realize how embarrassing that would be for me?"

She looked at me, disappointment replacing the pleased look she'd had seconds before. "I just wanted to make up for this morning. I should have wished you a happy birthday first thing. I should have bought that cheesecake for you."

"You could have just left the cake out of the basket. We could have had it later. With Dad. In *our* home."

"I don't know. The idea just popped into my head. I thought it'd be cute."

"Cute?" I stopped and put my hands on my hips. "That wasn't cute. They probably think we're crazy!" I realized the second it slipped out of my mouth that I'd said the wrong thing.

Anger flashed across her face. She turned and jogged through the lawn and into the house. Just as I got inside, the kitchen door slammed and I heard the garage door going up. *I should go after her.* I walked upstairs.

"What was that?" Dad came out of his office.

"I said the wrong thing, set her off." I went in my room and flung myself on the perfectly made bed.

"What happened?"

"She got the new neighbors to sing me Happy Birthday and served us all the housewarming-cake she'd bought for them. It was so embarrassing." I grabbed a pillow and put it over my head.

Dad laughed and I felt the bed shift as he sat. "So what exactly did you say that sent her storming out of here?"

I sat up and shook my head, guilt churning inside of me. "That they probably thought we were crazy."

He flinched. "Ohh, you hit that button."

"Where do you think she went?"

"The studio, I bet, but let me call her." He pulled out his cell and called.

"Where are you?" Dad asked. He looked at me and nodded. "Okay, just get back here by six so we can go out for Lola's birthday dinner."

"She's gone to the studio?" Mom rented a small space in the nearby art park. It was her refuge, a place to do what she loved without distractions. She'd been going there a lot since school got out. I was beginning to suspect why and it wasn't good.

"Yep, and by the time she gets back all will be well." Dad reached over and squeezed my shoulder. "Now, why don't you get to packing? Only two days till DC."

I was just pulling my suitcase down from the closet when the phone rang. I grabbed it from my nightstand. "Happy birthday," Hannah chirped.

"Thanks. How's it going there?"

"Ah, you know. My dad's a dork and my stepmom's a bore. But she did take me shopping and bought me some amazing strappy sandals."

"That's cool, I guess."

"I met this hot guy named Jase at the pool yesterday. He's supposed to text me."

"Nice," I replied.

"So what's going on with you? Any excitement on your birthday?"

"Sort of. I met the new kid across the street. He goes to Washington."

"What's his name? Is he cute?"

"I don't know if you'd think so, but I kinda do. His name's Ian White."

"Don't tell me. Was he wearing skinny jeans?"

I sat down on the bed. "Yes."

"Oh gross, Lola. That guy is not cute. He's a freak."

My face got hot. "How do you even know who he is? I've never seen him at school."

"Last year, he hung around with that weirdo, Jacob, with the spider tattoo. I mean, who gets a tattoo on their neck? And a spider, yuck!"

"You can't judge him by who he hangs out with. Imagine what people think when they see me with you," I joked to cover up my anger.

"Whatev. You know I make you look good." Someone yelled in the background on Hannah's end. "Hey Lo, I gotta go. We'll talk later. Don't get too cozy with the freak."

Sometimes Hannah made me want to scream. She could be so judgmental. But she had her share of issues, too. We'd first met in the third grade in the waiting room at the child psychologist's office. She was there because of her dad's alcoholism and I was there because of Mom's bipolar disorder. That was back when Mom was really bad and, needless to say, Hannah could relate. Her dad kicked the booze, but my mom would always be bipolar. Over the years, we had less and less in common. Still, we stayed friends.

I finished packing for the trip and tried to call Mom. She must have turned off her cell because the call went straight to voicemail. "Just wanted to apologize for before. I was just embarrassed. Maybe after dinner tonight, we can watch a movie or something. I love you."

I should have never uttered the word crazy in her presence. Dad banned that word from my vocabulary when I was in second grade and Mom had to check in to the psyche hospital for attempted suicide. She'd always had dramatic mood swings, but that was when she hit rock bottom, and the diagnosis came in. She'd been mostly okay since then, only a few relapses when she couldn't take the side effects of her meds.

I took the vacuum out and plugged it in. Forget fighting the urge. It was hopeless. After the perfect carpet lines were made, I stretched out on the bed and grabbed *The Diary of Anne Frank* off the table. Before long, my eyelids were heavy. Maybe, by the time I woke up, Mom would be home.

The train comes to a complete stop. The soldiers open the doors to the cars. Snow falls. I lift my head and feel the cold, wet flakes land on my face. If this were another time, I might stick out my tongue. Instead I hold back tears. Mother reaches and takes my hand. The soldiers bark orders as they herd the crowd toward the cars. Papa puts his arms around Mother and me as we inch closer to the train. The young soldier stands at the edge of the car we're closest to, a rifle over his left shoulder, and helps people step in. He glimpses into the eyes of each person. Nazis think we Jews are wretched, undeserving of even eye contact, so why does this boy risk it? What is he trying to see? When it's my turn, he takes my hand and hoists me up. His eyes are the color of the grassy meadow where I used to play, and when I look into them, my own sadness and fear reflect back to me. I want to ask his name, find out how he ended up here, and learn where he'd be if he had the choice. Me? I'd be in school with Sarah.

"Lola, wake up!" Dad called from the bedroom door. "It's six-fifteen and your mom's not here yet. I can't get her on her cell. We could go out, just the two of us, or I could call in a pizza."

I was shaken by the dream. It was just as real as the last one I'd had—like I really was that girl. Hearing Mom wasn't back yet made me feel even worse. "Pizza is fine." I rolled over, inhaled deeply and tried to conjure up a happy memory.

"I'll go order it."

I nodded, but didn't say a word. I didn't want him to know I was crying. I heard his footsteps going down the stairs. He should have been more worried than that. I was. I was also angry. It wasn't like Mom to forget my birthday and blow off family traditions. We always celebrated birthdays the same way, with dinner at Tony's. Had I upset her so much that she didn't want to be with me? I had the sick feeling that things were changing, and not in a normal way.

It was eight-thirty when Mom walked through the door. Dad and I were on the couch watching a movie, a box of cold pizza sat in front of us on the coffee table. "I am sooo sorry! I got caught up in a collage I was working on and completely lost track of time. I only realized how late it was when it started getting dark out." Mom sat down on the other end of the sectional.

She looked like she'd been crying all day. I never meant to hurt her that much. It was so stupid of me to let that word slip.

"We didn't go to Tony's." I leaned up and pushed the pizza box toward her. "We left some for you." I looked back at the TV.

"I'll make it up to you. You and I can go shopping in DC, and then we'll go someplace nice, do your birthday dinner there."

Dad stopped the movie. "Today's her birthday, Christine. We

had plans for today and you screwed them up." Hearing his angry tone scared me.

"I know, Nick. I'm sorry. I said I was sorry already. I wasn't thinking straight today. What do you want me to do?" Mom stared at Dad.

"Are you taking your meds?"

Mom stood up and walked into the kitchen. I knew what that meant.

Dad stormed after her. "I gather your silence means no!"

A cabinet opened and slammed closed. I jumped at the sound.

"No, alright? No! I'm not taking my meds. I got sick of feeling numb and empty and not being able to paint," Mom yelled back.

I pulled my legs to my chest, wiping tears on my knee. I knew Mom wouldn't forget my birthday unless something was off.

"How long?" Dad asked. I listened for the answer.

"A few weeks," she replied. "After the school year ended. I just wanted to see if I could do it. It's been a long time, Nick. Maybe I'm alright."

"It doesn't go away Christine. You keep it at bay with the meds. You won't be alright. None of us will be."

His words hit me like a brick. None of us would be alright if Mom wasn't. Was that true? I got up and walked to the doorway. I wanted to remind them I was there.

"How would you know? Huh?" Mom's voice cracked. "I don't even see you anymore. We pass in the kitchen, getting coffee, and the rest of the time you're in that office, glued to your computer. You haven't even slept in our bed for a week."

"Just because I've been busy lately—and that's all it is, work picking up—doesn't mean I can't see your patterns. We've been down this road before. You throw yourself into your art, or whatever it may be in the moment, and completely forget about

Lola and me. Then you crash hard, taking us down with you." He got quiet. "I can't do this again."

"What are you saying, Nick?" I saw the fear in Mom's eyes.

"I'm saying I'm tired." Dad turned to leave, bumping into me on his way out of the room. "Sorry, Lola." He reached back and squeezed my shoulder.

I walked to the table where Mom sat sobbing over a glass of wine. Dread began to build inside of me. If she was off her meds, what was going to happen? The last time she said she'd be fine, but it didn't end up that way. What would happen this time? I needed her to be okay and Dad to start paying attention.

"I love you, Mom." I walked behind her and wrapped my arms around her. "I don't care about what happened today. I just want you to be alright."

"Thank you, baby." She kissed my hand.

"You want to come watch the movie with me? We can start it over."

"No, I'm pretty tired. I think I'll just call it a night." Mom took the wine bottle and her glass and went to the bedroom. Their room was right off the kitchen and when the door shut, I sat down at the table and cried. My fifteenth birthday was officially the worst one ever.

I checked in on Dad on the way to my room, found him staring at the computer screen, a smile on his face. I stopped in my tracks. "I guess you're not worried about Mom?" I asked from the doorway, feeling scared.

He pushed away from his desk, replaced the smile with a serious face. "There's nothing I can do about it right now. We just have to wait and see."

"Is that work?" I pointed to the computer.

He shifted in his seat. "Yeah."

"Guess I'll leave you to it then." I reached for the doorknob. "You want me to shut this? I'm going to my room to listen to some music."

"Sure." He nodded. "Happy birthday. I love you," he called as I closed the door.

"Sure," I said under my breath. On the way to my room, I stopped in the bathroom and stared in the mirror. My brown eyes were a little bloodshot, but otherwise there was no indication that I'd been crying. I guess that's why Dad didn't bother to ask if I was upset . . . I didn't look it. Just like he didn't.

Chapter 4

The two-hour nap before dinner coupled with parental drama made it impossible to sleep. Pacing by the window, I looked out and noticed a figure sitting on the tailgate of the green truck across the street. In the dim light of the streetlamp, I recognized Ian. He was looking toward the sky, tracing the constellations maybe. I remembered the way he'd smiled at me and I wanted to go to him, get to know him. I'd been watching for a few minutes when he saw me at the window and gestured for me to come out. It was one in the morning and I doubted either of my parents was still awake. I could easily walk out the front door and join him. The dread I'd carried most of the day turned to happy anticipation at the thought of sitting next to him on that truck under the stars. I'd never snuck out of the house before, never had a reason to. Although, was it really sneaking out if I was just going to the end of my driveway?

I crept into the hall and put my ear up to Dad's office door. He was snoring. I headed downstairs to their bedroom and peeked in on Mom. She slept sprawled across the bed, the empty wine bottle and glass on the nightstand next to her. I stepped in and put my hand on her back. I wasn't exactly sure how drunk a person got from a whole bottle of wine. A couple of minutes of listening to her breathe convinced me she was okay. I headed for the front door, hoping Ian was still outside.

Before I stepped out, I took one last look in the decorative mirror by the front door. My hair, normally straight, hung in waves over my shoulders. I ran my fingers through it, wishing I'd bothered with the flat iron. I hated what the muggy southern summers did to my hair. I pulled at my Washington High t-shirt, stretching it to cover my legging-clad backside. I gently turned the knob and crept out the front door, despite the wave of anxiety that flooded me.

"I wasn't sure if you could see me." Ian stood up as I approached the truck.

I shrugged. "Yeah, thanks for the invite. Couldn't sleep." I pointed to my bedroom.

"Yeah, me neither. It was a busy day. I'm wired."

"You all moved in?" I sat on the tailgate of the truck. Ian sat beside me.

"Basically, just have to get a few more things from my mom's place. What about you? Did you have a good birthday?"

A nervous laugh escaped me. "Not really."

"Anything you want to talk about?" Ian's voice was kind, inviting.

I shook my head.

He nudged me with his elbow. "Aww, come on. It always feels better after you share."

"I don't know where to start. It was a weird day."

"Weird is good. Tell me more."

I hesitated for a moment, but the curious look in his eyes won me over. "Well, I had the same creepy-real dream twice, my mom bailed on my birthday plans after embarrassing the heck out of me in front of you guys, and then tonight, she and my dad got into it."

"I'm sorry. If it helps any, you got no reason to be

embarrassed. I thought your mom was nice."

"Ugh!" I put my hands over my face and laid back.

"I take it you'd rather not discuss your mom. Tell me about this dream of yours then."

I sat back up and looked at him. "Really?"

"Yeah, sure. Maybe I can analyze it for you. I'm good at that crap."

"All right." I pulled my legs up and locked my hands around them. "In the dream, I'm a Jewish girl. I'm with my mom and dad and a whole bunch of other Jews. I know that 'cause we're all wearing the Star of David. We're standing at a station. It's cold and snowing, and a train is coming in. Nazi soldiers are there and when the train stops, they open the doors and we all climb in."

"Whoa." Ian shook his head. "That's some heavy stuff."

"There's also this one soldier and I can't help but notice him. He's treating us like humans. I can tell he doesn't want to be there. As strange as it sounds, I feel his fear as much as my own."

"And it felt real?"

I nodded. "As real as sitting here right now."

"Hmmm." Ian stood up and paced a few steps, his back to me. "Maybe it was a past-life memory."

I got a sick feeling in my stomach. "A what?" The words came out shaky.

Ian turned and looked at me for a moment. Then he cracked a wide smile. "I'm just kidding, Lola. Was there anything you watched or read that could make you dream this?"

"I have been reading Anne Frank."

"Well, there you go."

Relief washed over me, though Ian seemed more uncomfortable. He'd made a joke and I didn't get it. How did I miss that?

"How long ago did your parents split?" I scrambled to change the subject.

"Two years."

"And how often will you be here?" I pointed to his house.

"Every other week"

"That's a lot of back and forth."

"Yeah, but it's worth it. So many fathers just get their kids on the weekends. I'm glad they didn't do it like that."

"Your parents sound cool."

"Yeah, they're alright." Ian looked at his watch. "It's real late. You sure it's okay for you to be out here."

"Probably not, but I figured they wouldn't notice."

He smiled and looked right into my eyes. "You risked getting busted to hang with me?"

"Something like that."

"So, I wasn't just a weird guy you met on your weird birthday?"

"I don't think you're weird." I looked down at my feet, remembering what Hannah had said about Ian.

He reached out his hand to me. "Good, 'cause I can always use more allies."

I reached back and put my hand in his. It was warm and soft.

"I'm going to my mom's tomorrow, but maybe we can hang out when I get back next Saturday."

"We're going to DC from Sunday to Sunday, but after that, definitely." My hand fell to my side. "I guess I'll get back home now. Thanks for the chat."

"No problem." He waved as I walked away.

On our first day in DC, Dad suggested we visit the Holocaust Museum. He'd noticed me reading *The Diary of Anne Frank* and thought I'd appreciate it. As we entered the museum, I felt almost guilty for the fascination that welled within me. I'd seen pictures in books of the ditches filled with corpses and Anne Frank's experience was still fresh in my mind. It was horrific, yet it lured me. I wanted to take in the details, understand the darkness. Yet, at the same time, I felt sick for having that desire. I looked at Mom and Dad. They seemed to be equally called to by this place. Quietly, we looked at the exhibits and took in the power of these tragic events. I wondered if the dreams I'd had were related to this.

We walked through an exhibit showing a re-creation of the Auschwitz prison camp. There was a wall of wooden bunks and next to it was a picture of men with sunken faces crowded into bunks just like the ones on display. Dad stood before the photograph and tears flowed. He fought them back at first, wiping his eyes quickly with the back of his hands and pulling a tissue from his pocket for his nose. Finally, he just slid down against a wall and put his arms and forehead on his knees. The way his body shook, it was impossible to hide the fact he was weeping. Mom slid down next to him on the floor, gently putting her hand on his shoulder. Several people walked by them. They pointed and whispered. Dad continued to cry. It was the first time I'd ever seen my father cry and I didn't want to be embarrassed by it, but I was. No one else in the room was weeping.

I sat on a bench across the room and waited for it to end. When his tears finally stopped, he stood and walked to the next room. Mom walked over and reached for my hand. I took it and together we followed him.

"What was that?" I whispered to her while Dad was reading the next display.

"I don't know. I've never seen him like that." She gazed at him, her eyes soft. "It was beautiful."

"It was weird," I replied.

"Lola! Do you not understand how important it is for us to purge our emotions?" Her eyes were locked on me now. I looked away. "Release keeps us physically healthy. Your father holds too much in. Why do you think he's always creaking around the house like an old man?"

"I just thought it was because he's up all hours of the night and always falling asleep on the couch." I shrugged. She shook her head and joined Dad.

We left the museum at five in the afternoon. There was still more to see but it was nearing closing time and we were hungry and emotionally drained. On the way back to the Metro, I walked next to Dad. Mom trailed behind us, distracted by the sites and people.

"Are you feeling better now?" I hadn't mentioned his moment until now.

"Actually, yeah. Your mom has always said she feels much better after a good cry. Now I get it."

"Why did you cry?"

"The weight of it all." He shook his head, seemingly searching for a better answer. "It felt like I was bearing the load of all that loss and grief, like I'd been there myself."

"Weird." Ian's joke from the other night flashed in my mind.

"You ain't kidding." He put his arm around me and turned back to Mom. "Come on, Christine. Here's our station."

We made our way down to the platform. It was packed. "Looks like we're just in time for rush hour," Mom said.

The train pulled in and we pushed ourselves into the heap of people and boarded. The doors closed right behind us. Mom and Dad knew where we were going. I didn't. I'd been too excited to keep track of the stops on our way to the museum. Sweat dripped down my face, starting at my forehead and slowly traveling along my hairline. White spots danced in front of my eyes. I closed them, counted my breath. It was quick and shallow. I tried to breathe deeply. I couldn't. I opened my eyes. The spots were worse. I searched for an empty seat. There was none.

"Lola, are you okay?" Dad snapped a finger in front of my eyes. The sweat dripped off my chin. The voices all around me sounded echoey and far off. Soon they were all just white noise, even my dad's words. I closed my eyes once more. All I could hear was the train.

My eyes are closed. A man near me is saying a prayer. He repeats it, over and over. It is a prayer for protection. I open my eyes. I'm packed in tightly between my parents and two neighbors. My mother looks up to my father, a hand resting on her stomach. She's larger than most women. I follow her gaze just as my father looks down at me.

"We'll be fine. I promise," he says.

"Can you really make that promise?" I ask.

He kisses the top of my head. Tears well in his eyes. My mother's face is blank. She's no longer looking at Papa, just staring into space.

I look around us. So many people crowded into such a small space. It is both hot and cold. The air at the top is cold. A draft travels through grates in this train car. A hint of light travels through one small window, letting me know it is still day time. Though I sense where we are headed, no one has told us.

The train car is eerily quiet for a place that holds so many people captive. I scan the faces in the crowd. Some are familiar, but not all. Many hold empty gazes, like Mother's. Occasionally, there is an exhausted moan, a sniffle or cough, but mostly we just sit listening to the man's prayers. He is saying them for all of us.

There isn't room for everyone to sit at once. We are lucky enough to be relieved by some fellow passengers who stand after some time, allowing us to sit. Space is that scarce. Sitting offers a different perspective. Our aching bodies are relieved, but our senses are tortured. The stenches of urine and worse engulf us. Next to us, a woman holds her sick, or maybe dying, child. I can't tear my eyes away. The mother rocks in the small space available and silently weeps. The child never moves. My heart aches more than the empty pit in my stomach. It's been so long since we last had a meal.

"Is there food?" I ask Mother.

"They have promised us soup upon our arrival."

"Arrival where?"

"I am not entirely sure." She lifts her arm and places it around my shoulder. I fix my gaze upon the star on her sleeve. The yellow Star of David. I look at my father. It is on his arm as well. All around me, every person is marked with the yellow star.

"What are they going to do to us?" I ask, my voice rising. My heart pounds. A sense of urgency surges within me. "We have to get out of here!" I scream and grab Mother's hand, trying to stand up. I can't rise. I reach up and pull at the person beside me. Instead of helping me up, she falls on top of me. I claw and scream.

"Get hold of her!" a man yells from nearby.

"Darling, please. Calm down."

"They're going to kill us!" I wail. "Open the doors. We must get out of here." I throw myself into the crowd. My father pulls me back.

"GET HOLD OF HER!" The man is louder this time.

My father hugs me tightly. I jerk and kick.

"Do it, or I will," the man says. I see him push his way toward me. He stares right into my father's eyes. I want to stop the screams but I can't. The man raises a fist. Everything goes black.

I woke to the stench of smelling salts, an EMT standing over me. I turned my head and saw Dad on my right. "They're going to kill us, Papa," I mumbled.

He put his hand on my forehead. "Sweetie, it's okay. You passed out on the train, that's all."

"We're not on the train?"

"No, we carried you off at the first stop." Mom reached for my hand.

"They were taking us somewhere and I just knew it was bad." I tried to sit up. My head was pounding. "He hit me. I can't believe you let him hit me." I looked at Dad.

"What are you talking about? No one hit you. You passed out. Your mother caught you. You didn't even touch the ground."

I lifted my hand to my cheek. "This man hit me. I was scared, that's all."

"You must have had a hallucination, baby." Mom rubbed the back of my hand. Someone handed me a bottle of water. I drank.

"You want us to take her in?" The EMT looked at my parents. He looked familiar, a lot like the man who hit me. I must have seen him somehow, transferred his face to the dream.

My parents looked at me. "You think you'll be all right?" they asked.

"I just need to finish this water. Then I can get up."

"Are you sure?" Dad looked closely at my eyes. I nodded. "We'll be okay. Thank you." He stood up and shook hands with the medic.

"We're sorry for the trouble," Mom added.

"It's no problem, ma'am. In this heat and these crowds, it tends to happen." He gathered his gear. "You all have a good day now. And you feel better." He smiled at me. I felt a shudder down my spine.

Chapter 5

It was hard to enjoy the rest of the vacation when all I could think about was where I'd gone when I passed out. It was too powerful, too real. And the hallucination, as my mom referred to it, seemed to pick up where the dreams left off. In the first dream, we were waiting for the train. In the second, we were boarding it. I had some kind of TV show going on in my subconscious. This was not normal. What did it mean and how could I make it stop? I needed to figure this out before the next episode.

The last night in our hotel, Mom and Dad crashed early. I sat dazed in my bed, some money show on CNN lighting the room, wondering which way my life was veering. I wanted those dreams I'd had to just be dreams. But there was more going on. I knew it. Maybe I could handle it better if things weren't so off with my parents . . . and if I wasn't feeling so drawn to the one person my best friend told me to stay away from. All the scenarios in my mind made me anxious. I buried my head in the pillow and cried.

"Lola. What's wrong, honey?" Mom placed her hand on my cheek. I hadn't even heard her get up.

"I'm scared." I rolled over to face her.

"There's nothing to be afraid of, I'm here."

"It just feels like things are changing and that thing on the train, the hallucination, is a part of it."

"It wasn't real. It can't hurt you." She sat on the edge of the bed.

"It felt so real, I'm surprised I don't have a bruise." I put my finger on the place where I'd been hit.

"Go to sleep. It'll all be better in the morning." She pulled away, lifted herself out of bed. I reached up for her hand.

"Don't leave, Mom. Sleep with me. Please."

She snuggled behind me. I concentrated on the warmth of her arms around me until I drifted off to sleep.

The next morning, we had a huge breakfast at the hotel buffet before heading to the airport. Dad had his phone out, texting or tweeting.

"Must you do that at the breakfast table?" I said jokingly as he moved his pudgy fingers across the small screen.

"Sorry, work stuff." He glanced at me, but kept using the phone.

"Not Twitter?" I asked.

He shook his head, but didn't look up.

Mom lifted her orange juice glass into the air, oblivious to the mention of Twitter and what it meant. "Here's to another Ray family vacation!"

I picked up my glass and we both stared at Dad.

"Oh." He scrambled to put the phone down and grabbed his glass. "Here here!"

My anxiety grew as we traveled home. I wondered what would happen when we returned to the real world. Would Dad retreat to his office and ZanyZandria? Would Mom keep it together or fall back into the old patterns that the medicine kept at bay? Would Hannah freak if I told her I liked Ian? And most of all, would I have another episode like the one on the Metro?

When we pulled into our driveway, the first thing I noted was what was missing across the street. No green truck meant no Ian. I wished he was home. I was dying to talk to him about what happened and what I'd seen.

I paced in my room for a bit then vacuumed over the tracks I'd made. Ian still wasn't back, so I decided to call Hannah. Maybe I could tell her about the dreams and the hallucination. She might have some ideas. I grabbed the phone.

"Hey, I'm back from the trip."

"Oh, my gosh. I've been dying to talk to you, Lo! So I ended up going out with that guy, Jase, and you wouldn't believe where he took me."

"Where?" I asked, hoping that after her story, she'd listen to mine.

"A parking lot."

"A what?"

"A freakin' parking lot. He took me to a Big Lots parking lot where a bunch of his friends sat and drank beer that they stole from their parents' fridges."

I could imagine Hannah's eyes rolling as she spoke. "Oh, my gosh. You didn't drink beer, did you?" I thought of all the times she swore she'd never drink like her dad.

"I took a sip. It tasted like vomit," Hannah paused. I started to speak but was interrupted. "Anyway, when he took me home, he went in for a kiss and I totally turned my head away. He ended up kissing my hair. It was so funny."

I imagined the poor guy's face. It wasn't funny. "I don't suppose you saw him again."

"He keeps calling, but I've been ignoring him. I defriended him on Facebook today. I hope he notices and gets the message."

"Well, we had an interesting family vacation." I couldn't wait to finally talk about what happened, see what Hannah thought.

"That's nice. We're going to the beach next week. It's going to be awesome. My step-cousin's going and she is totally gorgeous. Guys flock to her. I'm thinking I'm sure to meet a hottie or two hanging around with her."

"Sounds fun." Deflated, I decided not to bother. Ian could hear the story later.

"Oh, it definitely will be." Hannah got quiet for a moment. I could hear a clicking sound, probably from her iPad. "Anything new with the freak across the street?"

"Not really," I lied.

"That's a relief. I was afraid you were going to say you've been hanging out with him all week."

"Nope, already said I was on vacation." I let out a frustrated sigh.

A chime sounded on Hannah's end. "You sound tired, I'll let you go." She probably just needed to answer a Facebook message.

"Okay, talk to you later." I hung up feeling even worse than before I'd called her. Aren't you supposed to be able to talk to your best friend about anything? It seemed I could never get a word in edgewise with Hannah, unless it was gossip of some sort. I was going to go crazy if I didn't talk to someone. I walked to the window just in time to see Ian cross the street.

I was on my way downstairs when the doorbell rang.

"Lola, you want to get that?" Dad called from his office.

"Got it!" I called back as I opened the door. Ian was standing in front of me wearing baggy shorts and holding his skateboard. It was the first time I'd seen him in shorts and his thin, pale legs were actually quite cute.

"Saw that you were back," he pointed to the car in the driveway, "and thought I'd stop over, say hi."

"Hi," I replied as an awkward silence set in. Ian swayed back and forth still clinging to his skateboard. "Would you like to come in?"

He looked over my shoulder, into the house and then at his watch. "I would, but I'm on my way out to the skate park. Will you be home tonight?"

I nodded.

"Would you like to meet, like before?"

"Sure that'd be nice." I swatted at a mosquito that was trying to fly into the house.

Ian's shoulders relaxed, a smile crossed his face. "Can you get out around ten?"

I nodded again. "I'll figure it out."

"Cool. I'll see you later then." He dropped the skateboard on the sidewalk and stepped on it. "Now close that door before you get anymore invaders."

I waved and closed the door, leaning against it to savor the moment. He wanted to hang out with me. I'd never had a boyfriend or even a friend that was a boy. I'd kissed a boy once, on a trip to the beach with Hannah, but whatever this thing was with Ian, it was a first for me. And even better, I knew he'd listen to me and that I could tell him all about what happened on the Metro.

Around ten, I looked out the window. Ian wasn't out yet. I paced back and forth next to the bed. My stomach flipped. I opened the closet, touched the vacuum. Normal, normal, normal, I thought to myself as I resisted the urge to use it. Dad was working in his office and Mom had gone to bed early. Ian would be out there at any moment. I didn't know if I should wait for Dad to fall asleep or if he'd even notice I was gone at all. After being away for a week, it was a safe bet he'd be burning the midnight oil, so waiting for him to fall asleep was out of the question. I stepped into the bathroom and fumbled around, trying to make noise so Dad would think I was getting ready for bed. After an adequate amount of time pretending, I opened the door to his office.

"Working hard?" I asked as I stepped into the room.

"Not really. Got stuck on something, so now I'm just blowing off steam on Twitter."

The fact that he admitted to being on Twitter gave me hope that my worries about ZanyZandria were unnecessary. Would he be so open about it if he was doing something bad?

"I don't really like Twitter." I looked over his shoulder and saw her name flash on the screen.

"I think you get into it once you get a good group. These folks I stumbled on, crack me up with their conversations."

"Who's ZanyZandria?" I started to shake a little, Goodnight Dear trailed through my mind.

"Oh, she's just the resident flirt," he laughed, reading her tweet.

"Does she flirt with you?" I clasped my hands together.

I noticed his neck turn red. "She flirts with everyone."

I patted him on the head. "Well, she better stop flirting with you or she'll have me and Mom to deal with." I laughed to pretend it was a joke.

Dad laughed too, though it sounded forced. "You going to bed?" he asked.

"Yeah, just came in to say goodnight. What about you?"

"Plan to hang here until I have a burst of inspiration or fall asleep, whichever happens first."

"See you in the morning then." I leaned down and kissed him on the cheek. "I love you."

"Love you too."

I left his office, shutting the door behind me. I walked back to the window in my room, thinking about ZanyZandria. Before the thoughts could carry me too far, I spotted Ian rolling back and forth on his skateboard between our two driveways. I put a few throw pillows under the covers on my bed and turned on the noisemaker I use sometimes when I can't sleep. I stood back to survey my work. If Dad happened to peek in on me, in the dark, it would look like I was in bed. I turned the knob as I closed the door, listening for the small click that indicated it was really shut, and tip-toed down the steps. I made it all the way to the front porch without so much as a tiny creak from the floors.

Once outside, I sprinted through the yard to the road, startling Ian so much he fell off the skateboard.

"Jesus!" He whisper-shouted.

"Oh, my gosh. I'm so sorry." I took his hand and helped him up.

A dark curl fell across his forehead from beneath the fedora. I was overcome by the urge to push it back into its place under the hat. It wasn't my OCD either. The thought of such an intimate act, touching his face, rattled me . . . in a good way, a way I'd never felt before.

"I was just beginning to wonder if you were having second thoughts." Ian's voice pulled me back to the moment.

I walked over and sat down in the driveway. "Second thoughts about what?"

Ian followed me. "I don't know. Sneaking out," he paused, "hanging with me."

I had no second thoughts about sneaking out or seeing Ian, but I was very aware that I should have. I'd learned enough about Ian to know that he wasn't exactly normal. If my intention truly was to feel like I belonged with Hannah and her group at school, making friends with him was not the best choice. "The sneaking out part was a little nerve wracking, but you? No way," I twisted a string hanging from my shorts, "I've been looking forward to this all week." My heart nearly beat out of my chest. I'd never said anything like that to a boy before. Where did the confidence come from?

"Me, too." He nodded as a satisfied smile crossed his face.

"How was your week?" I asked.

"I discovered a new fashion statement." He held both wrists in the air. They were covered in plastic bracelets. "Silly Bandz! What do you think?"

I laughed. "Are you serious?"

"I'm dead serious." He stared at me, trying to keep a straight face. "These are genius. You see, on my wrists right now is an array of fruits, animals, and princesses." He imitated one of those spokespeople from the shopping network. "I don't know how I could have undervalued the beauty and style back when they first came out."

I shook my head, laughing harder now. He took off a bracelet and shot it through the air. It hit me on the forehead. "Ow!" I rubbed my head.

"Sorry. Can you pass that back to me? I have to return the collection to Sammy's room before he notices it's gone."

"So you won't be wearing those to school next year?"

"Nah. Just wanted to make you laugh."

"You are funny."

"You're kind." He smiled at me. "Now tell me, how was our Nation's Capital this week?"

"You won't believe what happened."

"Do tell."

I finally got to tell the story of what happened on the Metro. I told him about how I passed out in the crowd and woke up on another train and in another crowd. I described the familiar faces and the stars on our clothing. I emphasized the man who hit me and how strange it was that he looked like the medic who helped me when my parents took me off the train. Ian studied me as I spoke. At one point, I noticed goosebumps on his arms. I told him how the hallucination seemed to pick right up where the dreams on my birthday had left off. I wondered aloud if it was haunting me and how long I would keep seeing it.

When I was done talking, Ian reached over and squeezed my

hand.

"What do you think?" I asked.

He shrugged his shoulders. "I have one theory, but honestly, I'm scared to tell you."

My heart dropped to my stomach. "Scared? Are you trying to freak me out? 'Cause it's working."

"No, no, no, I'm scared for myself. Of what you'll think of me."

I looked at him, puzzled.

"I mentioned it to you before and then I saw your face. You had that look in your eyes and so I pretended it was a joke."

"What are you talking about? What did you mention and what look did I have?"

"The night that you told me about your dream, I said it was a past life. Remember that?"

I nodded, remembering. "You were joking about that."

"No, I pretended to be joking when I saw your face. You looked at me like I should be in a straightjacket."

My chest felt tight. "I didn't look at you like that."

"Give me a break, Lola. Don't you think I know that look by now? At school, I'm Ian, the freak. I get that look all the time."

"I think you're imagining things. I didn't look at you like that and that's not true about school." Despite my insistence, Hannah's words rolled through my mind.

Ian stood and began to pace. "How would you know? You didn't even recognize me at all."

"I did recognize you." *But not from school.*

"You don't know what it's like, having everyone think you're weird. I don't want you to ever look at me like that."

"I do know what it feels like, ya know." I looked up at him as he walked by me.

"Sure, it's really hard to be a cheerleader." Anger invaded his voice.

"Just because I made some stupid team doesn't mean anything." I shook my head and decided to tell him everything. "Did it ever occur to you that maybe I tried out in the first place as a desperate attempt to not be like me anymore?"

"I've seen you at school, Lola. You've got friends. You're a part of something."

"Whatever. Hannah Parker is a part of something and I have the privilege of being her sidekick."

"Still, it's more than what I've got." Ian looked at his watch. "Listen, I'm gonna go now. I didn't want to get into all of this and now I just feel like an idiot."

I stood up. "Are you sure?" My heart sunk. I didn't want to go.

Ian nodded.

"Okay," I said and reluctantly headed back across the street.

"I'm sorry, Lola," Ian called.

I stopped and turned around. "I appreciate your honesty and I hope you feel the same. I really do want to hear your theory about my dreams."

"Next time, I promise."

I carefully opened the front door and slipped inside. The meeting was a disaster. Not to mention, I still didn't have a clue as to what to make of the dreams and hallucination. I needed Ian's help, but would he ever want to hang out with me again?

Chapter 6

On Wednesday morning, I slept in until ten. When I noticed the time, I jumped out of bed and ran downstairs to find Mom. She'd promised to take me to the pool. Other than our trip to DC, I'd spent most of the summer at home entertaining myself while she was holed up in her studio, creating. With her art, it was all or nothing and the 'all' was always a symptom of mania.

When I walked through the kitchen, coffee was still in the pot. I lifted the carafe and took a whiff. Burnt coffee was not a good sign. She hadn't even made it out of bed to feed her caffeine addiction. I went into her room. The curtains were closed and she was stretched out, sound asleep, in the center of the king-size bed. A pill bottle was on the nightstand. I picked it up and read the label, a fresh refill of sleeping pills.

"Mom." I sat down and gently nudged her shoulder. She groaned and rolled over. "Are we still going to the pool?"

"Just let me sleep for one more hour," she mumbled.

I went into the kitchen and fixed a bowl of cornflakes. The dread began to rise inside of me. Almost six weeks into summer break and it appeared Mom was crashing. I hated when she got depressed. It was worse than her being in the studio twenty-four/seven. And with Dad distracted, who would take care of her? I just wanted a normal life. Swimming was most definitely off the agenda now. I needed to get out. Was Ian home?

I noticed his truck in the driveway on my way upstairs to get ready. We'd ended things on such an awkward note Sunday night. He'd been avoiding me ever since, I was sure of it. I decided I'd go over and break through the weirdness. Once I was ready, I made the bed and ran the vacuum to calm the anxiety that threatened to keep me stuck in my bedroom all day.

With a shaky hand, I rang the bell. Sammy flung open the door.

"Sammy!" Ian yelled as he came through the kitchen toward us. "You know you're not supposed to open the door! Oh, hey, Lola." His voice lightened when he saw me.

"Sorry, E," Sammy replied.

Ian playfully popped him with the dish towel he carried. "You just got to be careful, li'l bro. It could be anybody at the door. I gotta look through the peephole before we open it."

"I promise, next time," Sammy yelled as he bolted down the hall.

"He does this kind of thing all the time. I just can't get it through his thick skull. One night, my mom got stuck for an hour with some Jehovah's Witnesses because Sammy opened the door." Ian gestured me into the kitchen where he went back to drying dishes. "So, how you been?"

"I've been good. A little bored. My mom was supposed to take me to the pool today, but she's still in bed. I thought I might see if you were up for going."

He contorted his face into a look of exaggerated disappointment. "I'd love to, but I got to watch the kid."

"He could come with us."

"Nah. Truck's a two-seater and I'm only allowed to drive him to Mom's and a few other designated places anyway. Just got my license in April."

It was a legitimate excuse, but I still felt my heart sink. "Well, I gave it a try." I turned and walked back toward the front door.

"You could hang here, you know." Ian followed me, still drying a plate. "It's a little bit better than boredom."

"So, you're not mad at me?"

"What would I be mad at you for?" Ian laughed as he asked the question.

"I got such a strange vibe from you the other night. I thought when I left, you might not want to hang out with me again."

"You were fine. I was the idiot." He slipped into the kitchen, put the last dish in the cabinet and gestured me toward the living room. "Have a seat."

He sat on one end of the couch, I sat on the other. "You never got to tell me your theory."

"Have you had any more dreams?"

"No, but I can't stop thinking about the ones I've had."

"Do you believe in reincarnation?"

"What, like when I die, I might come back as a cat or something?"

Ian smiled. "I guess that's one way you can think of it, but not really what I mean. I personally think human souls are too big—no that's not the word. What's the word?"

"Strong?"

"No. Immense, maybe. But that's not it either. Ugh, can't think of it. But anyway human souls are too something to fit into an animal."

"I don't know if I believe in it. Honestly, I've never even thought about it before."

"Well, that's my theory. I'd say your dreams and hallucination were flashbacks to a past life."

I got chills. "So, say I believe this theory. Where was this past life of mine?"

"The Holocaust, maybe?"

I shook my head. "No, that's absurd. You have to remember, I was reading *The Diary of Anne Frank* before the dreams and the hallucination happened after we went to the museum. It can all be explained."

Now, Ian shook his head. "What you described sounds like those transport trains. You were actually experiencing it. Visiting a museum and reading a book can't make you experience something!"

"Why couldn't it? I mean, geez, my dad bawled like a baby in front of the exhibit there. It certainly made him feel something."

"So, maybe he shared that past life with you."

I thought about what Dad said in the museum, about how he felt like he'd actually been there and lived through it. "I just don't know about all of this, Ian."

"I get that. It's a really hard concept to wrap your head around. I personally love the idea of endless do-overs. I mean, look at me. My parents are divorced, I spend more time with my six-year-old brother than with kids my own age, and the thought of becoming an adult in this economy gives me panic attacks. I certainly hope I get another chance for a better existence, or that maybe I had a perfect life last go-round."

"Have you ever had dreams like mine?"

He shook his head. "But, my mom, she uses hypnotherapy in her practice and she's had patients go to past lives before. She believes in it."

I thought about the crowded train, the Nazi soldiers, and that feeling of terror I'd experienced. It didn't feel like a dream, but I didn't want to think about it. It'd been over a week since I'd seen or dreamed anything. Maybe it was all over and this whole conversation was pointless. "You know what? This is really fascinating and maybe I could believe in something like reincarnation, but my stuff, it wasn't real. I just know it wasn't real." I looked Ian directly in the eyes hoping to convince him I was telling the truth.

He got up and walked over to the bookshelf. He came back and tossed a book in my lap, *Many Lives, Many Masters,* and sat back down. "Check it out. This psychiatrist accidentally did a past-life regression on one of his patients. It changed his career and life. And if you ever want to talk to my mom about the subject, I'm sure she'd be cool with it."

I smiled and nodded. Ian smiled back. For the first time I noticed a dimple beneath his right eye.

"E, I'm hungry!" We hadn't even heard Sammy come into the room.

"Okay, li'l man." Ian stood up and put his hand on his little brother's head.

I looked at the book then clutched it to my chest. "I think I better head home now, so you guys can do your lunch thing."

"You're welcome to join us."

"No, that's alright."

"Enjoy the book." Ian walked me to the front door.

I walked across the street and into the quiet house. Dad, I assumed, was upstairs working and Mom was still in her room. I went in. The curtains were still drawn and the TV was on with the volume low. She was lying in bed, staring at the screen, but not really watching.

"Mom, have you eaten yet?"

"No."

"I'm going to make myself a sandwich. You want one?" I sat on the bed and brushed my hand across her face.

"No."

"How about I make you a milkshake or smoothie, something

to cool you off?"

"I'm okay."

"I love you." I kissed her on the cheek and left the room. Suddenly I wasn't hungry anymore. I just wanted to lie down and cry. It'd been almost two years since her last episode of depression. For so long, I was on guard, waiting for a relapse. It was just a few months ago that I'd allowed myself to believe she was really going to stay normal. So much for that. Instead of making lunch or giving in to the urge to lie down, I went into Dad's office.

The door was open, so I slipped in quietly. Over his shoulder, I could see the computer screen. On it was a headshot of a woman, a selfie she'd taken with a cell phone camera. She had dark brown hair and crystal blue eyes with thick eyelashes. Her smile was full of joy. She looked familiar. Actually, her eyes looked familiar.

"She's pretty," I said. Poof, the screen was gone.

"You have to stop sneaking up on me like that, Lola." Dad was frazzled.

"Have you checked on Mom today?" I asked, though I was really wondering who the woman was. "She's starting again."

"I've got to get my work done."

"You weren't working just then. At least you could have taken her some food."

"What do you want me to do, force-feed her?"

"I want you to be nice to her and love her." I paused for a moment, holding back the tears. "I want you to love her enough that she'll get out of bed."

"I've tried that, Lola. You know it. It doesn't work." He pushed back from his desk and looked right in my eyes. "You know what? I want her to love me enough not to crawl back in there. I want her to turn it off and leave it off."

"She can't do that."

"She could if she kept taking the meds."

"When she takes the meds, she loses something."

"You don't seem to mind it when she's getting you places on time, making nice meals, and not embarrassing you."

"Can't you have some empathy?"

"I've had eighteen years of empathy." He placed his head in his hands. "Lola, I just don't know how many more I've got in me."

"What are you saying?"

"Nothing." He sighed. "I don't know."

I ran out of the room when I felt the tears coming. I didn't want him to see me cry. Dad had always been willing to help Mom through these rough patches. He'd make her favorite meals and coax her out of bed with all sorts of promises. Today, he hadn't even noticed she was still in bed. He was drifting away from her. He was drifting away from us.

I sat on my bed, staring at a painting on my wall. My head was spinning. Mom's depression, the weird dreams, Ian's theory, and my dad's strange behavior were too much to handle. I wanted it all to stop. Everything was going just fine until I turned fifteen and, just one week in, everything was so screwed up. I closed my eyes and breathed deeply.

My head pounds as I stare at the little window in the corner of the box car. I'm leaning on my mother's shoulder. She strokes my head and softly sings a lullaby. I listen to the song and realize I'm more helpless now than when I was an infant. Back then, I could at least scream. I've learned my lesson about screaming here, though. I won't dare to speak again. I'll just focus on the ray of light trailing through the window.

My head dropped forward and startled me awake. I only dozed for a second, but it was long enough to be that girl on the train again. I jumped up and grabbed my laptop. When the search screen appeared, I typed in "Holocaust trains" and clicked on images. The first picture I saw was one of an empty car with a rectangular-shaped window in the corner. It was exactly like the window I'd just stared at in my dream. I had to find out what I was seeing and why. Maybe if I answered those questions, I could figure out how to pull my parents back.

Chapter 7

By the weekend, things weren't looking much better with Mom. I'd been making her meals for days, but she was hardly eating. I convinced her to drive me to her studio by begging to see the collage she'd started on my birthday. It was there on the table, nearly complete, but left untouched for over two weeks. I'd brought the book that Ian gave me to the studio and I offered to let her work for a while. She declined.

"Do you want to talk?" I asked her in the car on the way home.

"He's going to leave me," she said in a near whisper, with her eyes focused on the road in front of us.

My stomach flipped. "He's going on a business trip, that's all." A lump formed in my throat.

She took her eyes off the road to glare at me. "For God's sake, Lola. I don't mean Tuesday."

"Daddy loves you. He won't leave."

"No, dear, Daddy only loves himself."

"That's not true. He loves me. He won't leave me."

"And there it is. The truth." Mom nodded her head as a tear slid down her cheek. "Perhaps he'll take you with him. Then you'll both be free."

I didn't say a word, just sat there holding back the tears. I didn't want to cry. I didn't want to show how weak I felt. I didn't want to be like her. But we'd felt the same thing. Both of us knew something had changed and my only hope was that we were wrong. If Dad left, I'd have to deal with Mom's depression on my own. I knew how to take care of myself when Dad was busy taking care of her, but I had no clue how I'd take care of the both of us. I wasn't strong enough to get her through this.

When we pulled into the garage, I let myself out of the car before Mom had even turned off the engine. I ran straight up to my room and crashed on my bed, thinking about how Mom was probably downstairs retreating straight to her bed, too. So many thoughts rushed through my head. I imagined Dad walking out the door. In the vision, I ran after him, threw myself around his legs like a little girl. He pried at my fingers, forcing me to let go. The thought of Mom and me alone, without Dad, scared me so much. For a fleeting moment, death seemed like a good solution. Better to lose my life than lose the only person who'd been a steady, loving, and constant presence in my life. As much as Mom loved me, she could never be steady and constant. But I refused to let the morbid thoughts overcome me. I looked around the room. It was already clean. I took the vacuum out of the closet and turned it on anyway. After much longer than necessary, I turned it off and put it away. Still, I needed something to do.

I walked into the hallway. Dad's office door was closed. I pushed it open and walked in. His sofa, now bed, was neatly made and his big black gym bag was missing. I wondered how long he'd been gone as I sat down in his chair in front of the computer. I moved the mouse around on the mousepad and watched the screen refresh in front of me. With a pang of guilt, I typed in the password space the name of the cat we'd had when I was little. I wondered if maybe Dad had changed it or if he even remembered that I knew it. The computer unlocked and I was staring at his gmail account. I wanted to learn something but I didn't know where to start. Before I could even make a decision, I heard the chiming sound of an instant message.

Z: Can't wait to see you on Wed.

Dad was taking a business trip to Austin in just a few days. Who was he going to see Wednesday? Maybe it was a client. But shouldn't exchanges with clients be more formal than this? Surely, Dad would figure it out if I replied. Yet, still, I couldn't fight the pull to know his plans for this trip.

Nick: Yes

Z: It is absolute kismet that your work is bringing you to me.

At least he wasn't lying about work. Unfortunately, it didn't make me feel any less sick to my stomach. I had to know more.

Nick: What do you have planned?

Z: Maybe a drive through the hill country, a nice dinner, and some live music.

I clicked the X in the corner. The screen vanished. What was Dad doing? And suddenly, I realized who Z was. ZanyZandria. It all made sense. The late nights, the obsession with Twitter and distance from Mom. He wasn't working. He was online dating. I'd never felt hatred toward my father. I wasn't sure I'd ever even been mad at him. Until now. My hands were shaking. I felt betrayed, disgusted. An image of him and ZanyZandria flashed through my mind. It made me want to throw up.

I heard Dad's footsteps on the stairs. I jumped out of his chair at the desk and began to tidy up.

"You cleaning the office?" Dad walked in and tossed his gym bag on the couch.

"Yeah, something like that," I mumbled and pushed past him out of the room. My heart was racing. I was so mad about what I'd learned. I shouldn't have gone digging. And what would he do when he opened that chat and saw what I'd done?

"That's no way to greet your old man," he called after me, happiness in his voice. "What did I do?"

More than you think I know. I went to my room and slammed the door. With my back pressed to the wood, I slid to the floor. I sat there for a while, not really knowing what to do or think. I'd never imagined anything like this before. My dad was supposed to be with my mom, no one else. I expected him to knock on my door to accuse me of being on his computer, but he didn't. I don't know what I would have done if he had. A part of me wanted to scream at him for betraying us. The rest of me just wanted to run away. I looked at the clock. Maybe Ian was home. I opened the bedroom door and peeked down the hall. Dad's office door was shut again. I bolted down the steps and out the front door just in case he wanted to interrogate me.

"Hey there!" Ian smiled when he opened the door. The smile quickly faded. "Are you alright?"

I tried to fight back the tears, but it was hopeless. He'd gone and asked that stupid question, the one that always opens the floodgates. I just shook my head. Ian reached for my hand and led me into the house.

"You want a Coke?" he asked when I sat down on the couch.

I shrugged, afraid that if I spoke I'd just sound like a blubbering mess. Ian nodded and walked to the kitchen. He was back a few seconds later, handing me a can of Coke. I popped it open and took a drink. The tears eased up.

"You want to talk about it?" he asked.

"I'm just a bit overwhelmed is all. Everything's a mess right now. My mom, my dad, and these crazy dreams."

Ian leaned toward me. "Did you have another dream?"

"I dozed for, like, a split second the other day and I was the Jewish girl again. I was staring up at the window of the train car. When I woke up, I Googled images from the trains and I saw a car with the exact window. I don't want to believe your theory, but it's starting to seem like the most likely answer."

"What were you doing right before you dozed?"

"Worrying about my parents and my life."

"So you were stressed?"

I laughed. "That's an understatement."

Ian leaned back for a moment, thinking. "It's a stress response!" He stood up, started pacing. "Think about it. Passing out on the Metro—that was your body's response to the stress of the crowd and heat. What about the other dreams? Were you worried about anything at those times?"

I thought back to the night before my birthday. I'd been fixating on all my issues, wondering how I could ever get control of the OCD and anxiety. I was thinking about the kids at school and if, even as a cheerleader, I'd really fit in. That was when I'd had the first dream. The second dream happened after Mom got mad and ran off to her studio. "Yeah, I was pretty much a wreck before both dreams."

"Now we know that the flashbacks aren't random."

"Great. As if I didn't have enough quirks, now I travel through time when I'm stressed." Tears welled in my eyes again. This was not normal. "Do you think this means I've got mental issues like my mom?" Asking the boy you have a crush on whether or not he thinks you're mentally unstable is not exactly a winning move. But still, I had to ask.

Ian moved closer and put his arm around me. It would've felt so nice if I wasn't so scared. "Everybody has their own issues, Lola. I believe that we're all here to learn and everything that comes to our life experience is there to teach us. There's a reason you're going back. You're going to be able to use what you're seeing to help you."

"So, what else should I know about reincarnation?"

He lifted his arm from around my shoulders and shifted his body to face me. "Karma is one part of it—the idea that what comes around goes around. If, in one life, you were dirt poor, in the next, you might be rich. If you were a killer in one life, you might be a healer in another."

"So, could that paramedic who helped on the Metro platform actually have been the man on the train who hit me during the hallucination?"

"I think so, for sure."

I thought about the people in my dreams. "The parents in that life feel like my parents now, but they don't look like them."

"We never look the same, but usually something is similar . . . eyes, a smile, or just the essence of someone."

"Essence?"

"Sometimes, you'd just know they were the same person by the way you feel in their presence."

"That's what it is with the dream parents. They just feel like my parents."

"Have you ever felt connected to someone in this life and you just can't explain why?" Ian asked.

I thought about Hannah and how connected I've always felt to her. Even though I doubt our friendship sometimes, I just know we belong together. "Yes, I have." I looked at Ian and remembered the urge I'd had to touch his face, how, despite Hannah's protests and my own desire to just be normal, I wanted to be friends with him. Maybe he's from a past life, too. That was a silly thought, though. Just an excuse to explain crushing on the wrong guy.

"Often, if you feel that strong connection then you were probably connected before. It's where the idea of soulmates comes from."

"So, there's truth to the idea that there's one soulmate out there for everyone?" I laughed.

"Not one, many. Some are more important than others, though."

"Well, that kind of takes the romance out of it."

"Romance is overrated." He leaned back and put his feet on the coffee table. A piece of paper fluttered to the ground. I reached down and picked it up.

"What's this?" On the paper was a drawing of a barcode with numbers underneath it.

"Well, I can't draw for crap but that's my tattoo design. I'm going to get it when I'm eighteen."

"Why are you working on it now if you're not getting it for two more years?"

"I don't know. It just came to me and I put it down. Been wanting a tat for ages and didn't know what I'd get until yesterday."

"What's with the numbers?"

"My birth date."

"Don't you think it's a bit insensitive to get numbers tattooed on you?"

"It's a barcode, Lola. It's a social statement about the gross materialism of our generation."

"I don't think any Holocaust survivors would find your social statement very clever. They had numbers tattooed on them, you know."

"I know that. I'm not stupid." Ian snatched the paper from me, folded it up and put it in his shirt pocket. "You take things way too seriously." He picked up the remote and flipped on the TV. I sat frozen, heart pounding in my chest.

He was right. I had taken it too seriously and personally. Everything I'd experienced lately had just made it real to me. The thought of those tragic events brought up so much anger and sadness within me.

"I'm sorry," I said when the urge to cry had receded. "It's not about me."

"Maybe it is about you."

"What do you mean?"

"You're flashing back to a past life—I know it—and you need to figure out what it's trying to show you."

I wanted to say he was ridiculous, but it wasn't feeling that way anymore. "How can I do that?"

"I'm going to my mom's tonight—she's making spaghetti. Will you come with me?"

"Is she going to hypnotize me or something?" I laughed.

"Not unless you've got some money and your parents' permission." Ian patted my leg. "But you can get her talking on the subject and maybe figure some stuff out."

"I don't know. Maybe your stress theory is wrong and it's just a fluke thing."

"Right, and that's why you just jumped all over me for wanting a tattoo of numbers."

"I said I was sorry. I just started learning about all of this, though, and it's a big deal. And knowing what I now know, that tattoo seems inappropriate."

"I didn't think about that when I drew it. It popped into my head, out of nowhere, and seemed so necessary."

"You're calling a tattoo necessary?"

"It sounds crazy, but yes. It feels like I have to do this someday." He pulled the paper out of his pocket and unfolded it. He placed it on the coffee table and we stared at it.

"I'll go meet your mom," I said still looking at the numbers.

"Really?"

"Yeah."

"I hope you don't think I'm a freak, but it just seems like you need some answers. I want to help you find them."

"Okay," I nodded and stood up. "What time should I be ready?"

"Six works for me." Ian followed me to the door.

Chapter 8

"Where have you been?" Dad yelled from the top of the stairs as soon as I walked in the front door. He hurried down and was in front of me, glaring at me, before I could even answer.

Being at Ian's had almost made me forget about the gmail chat this morning. Seeing Dad like this made it all come rushing back. He knew I'd been in his email. I could see it in his eyes. "I was over at my friend Ian's." I gestured toward the house across the street.

"What were you doing on my computer?" His voice was angry, but something else, too. Scared, maybe.

"It was already like that. I just sat down to clean." I looked down at my feet.

"Don't lie to me. It's password-protected."

"I needed to look something up. I didn't think you'd mind. You are the one who gave me the password."

"Did you find what you were looking for?"

I wondered if he'd seen the chat, if he knew how far I'd gone with it. Was he challenging me? Should I tell the truth? I banked on the theory that maybe Dad didn't want to talk about what I'd done or what I knew any more than I did. "No, you had too many windows open. I didn't want to mess anything up."

Dad stood frozen, his eyes locked on mine. The vein on the top of his head was pulsating. But he couldn't react. If he asked me anything else, he'd have to explain who Z was. He knew I'd replied to her though, I could see it in his eyes. He wouldn't be that angry at me just for using his computer.

"Is there anything else?" My voice was calm, though the rest of me was shaking.

"Yeah. If you plan on leaving this house, you need to tell me where you're going."

"Whatever," I mumbled under my breath as I ran upstairs to my room. In a few hours, Ian would arrive to take me to his mom's house. In the meantime, I picked up the book *Many Lives, Many Masters* and opened it. I'd been stuck on the first chapter ever since Ian gave it to me. Truth is I didn't want to read it, even believing in the past life theory didn't make me want to. I didn't want to delve deeper. I didn't want to complicate my life more than it already was. What difference did it really make if I'd been on one of those trains and arrived at some camp? It only helped me if it could make Mom get better and Dad stay. But Mom was in bed and Dad had one foot out the door. Zany-freakin'-Zandria. What had she done to him? I could feel the anger start to boil and rise. I grabbed a pillow and stepped into the closet. I knelt down in the corner, pressed the pillow to my face, and screamed with everything inside of me.

At five-forty-five, I made Mom a sandwich and took it to her room. "Here's a little dinner, Mom." I put the plate on the nightstand and sat down on the bed beside her, sadness falling over me as I noted her blank expression.

"Thank you." She didn't take her eyes off the TV.

I thought of what Dad said, his demand that I should tell him before I leave the house. Anger broke through my sorrow and I decided not to tell him anything. "Ian invited me to have dinner at his mom's house tonight. Is it okay if I go?"

"Uh, huh." Mom gave a slight nod. Had she even heard me?

I leaned over and kissed her shoulder. "I'll be home by 10:30." I checked my reflection in the mirror and left Mom's room. I opened the kitchen door and found the garage door was still up from Dad's trip to the gym. I looked back through the house. All was quiet. Dad was back upstairs working or chatting with Z. The thought of her flushed away any guilt as I crept through the garage and waited for Ian, leaning against Mom's Escape. When his green truck crossed the street, I made a run for it, meeting him just as he pulled into our driveway.

"What's the hurry?" He grinned as I climbed in, slightly out of breath.

"It's been a crappy afternoon. Can you get me out of here?"

Just as he put the truck in reverse, Dad stepped out onto the front stoop. "Where are you going, Lola?" I read his lips. His hands were in the air and his face looked confused and offended.

I rolled down the window. "Mom knows!" I yelled to him then whispered to Ian, "Just go." He put the truck in park.

Dad's face was red with anger when he reached the truck. "Well, you didn't tell or ask me. I thought we went over this earlier. You know she's checked out and in no condition to keep track of you."

"And you are?"

He ignored my question. "Where are you going?"

"I'm going to Ian's mom's house for dinner. I'll be back by ten-thirty. Mom said it was okay." I rolled up the window and looked at Ian. "Please go. I want to get out of here."

He gave a friendly wave in my dad's direction and put the truck in reverse. Dad watched us drive away with his arms folded over his chest.

"What was that?" Ian sounded shocked. "I thought you and

your dad were cool."

"Can you keep a secret?" I looked at him.

"Should I stop the car and get my Bible out of the glove compartment?"

I folded my arms and looked out the window.

"I'm sorry, Lola. Yes, yes, I can keep a secret. And I'm honored you feel like sharing with me."

"This is really serious, Ian. No more joking."

"I promise." He reached over and squeezed my hand.

"I'm pretty sure my dad's having an affair." My voice broke by the end of the sentence and tears began to fall.

"No way." Ian reached over and turned off the radio. I hadn't even noticed it was on.

"Yes, way."

"But he's always home, right?"

"It's an online affair." The sadness in my voice turned to anger. "Some Twitter flirt named ZanyZandria."

"Oh, Lola, I'm sure that can't be true. Your dad's a stand-up guy."

"It is true. I chatted with her."

"You did what?"

"I happened to be in his office, on his computer, when she sent him a message on gmail. I answered."

"Oh, my gosh. What did she say?" Ian slowed the truck. An angry driver whizzed by us.

"She lives in Austin."

"And . . ."

"Dad just happens to be going to Austin on Tuesday. They're going on a date! It's kismet!" I rolled my eyes.

"I'm so sorry, Lo." Ian reached over again and put his hand on mine. It felt good to have someone who would listen and care.

We pulled into the driveway of his mother's place a few minutes later. It was a brick two-story with ivy creeping up the walls.

"Do you still want to do this?"

I nodded my head while staring at the house. Another wave of grief was rising and I knew if I tried to speak or looked in his eyes, only sobs would come out. We opened our doors. They creaked with age.

I was here to talk about the dreams or flashbacks, my supposed visits to my past life in the Holocaust. Walking toward the house, I felt as though I was about to enter an enchanted cottage. Through this garage would be a fairy godmother. She'd have the answers to my questions about that far-off land or life I'd visited. But would any of it matter? In a few days, my father would be in the arms of some other woman, probably planning his escape from Mom and me. I really wasn't sure if any of this was going to help me but I was happy to be here, away from home, with Ian.

Ian pushed open the door and held out his hand for me to step inside first. I shook my head and pulled his elbow. "You first."

His mother stood at the stove stirring a pot of sauce. The room was filled with the aromas of garlic and basil. She tapped the side of the pot with the large spoon and placed it on the counter.

"Hi, Lola," she said reaching out a hand to me. "I'm so happy to meet you. Ian has told me a lot about you."

She was average height and size, with porcelain skin and dark, almost burgundy, red hair. I took her delicate-looking hand. "Nice to meet you, Ms. White."

"Call me Joan, please."

"Thank you for having me. I know it was kind of last minute." My hand throbbed slightly from her strong handshake.

"No problem at all, dear. If you want to go have a seat, dinner is almost ready." She pointed to the couch where Sammy sat completely engaged in his DS. "Samuel Jack, I told you to put that thing away ten minutes ago. Now turn it off and go clean up for dinner."

Sammy slowly rose from his seat, still pressing buttons and gazing at the small screen.

"Off, Sammy! Don't make me ask you again."

"Awwww, Mom!" He tossed the small machine onto the couch and shuffled toward the stairway. I sat down in the seat he'd left.

"You want me to hide this thing, Mom?" Ian picked up the portable game system and dangled it in the air. "Here's your chance."

"As tempting as that is, I must admit that sometimes my sanity relies on that contraption." Joan spoke over the sound of running water.

At that Ian plopped down on the couch. "All right, don't say I never offered to do anything for my brother." He leaned over and whispered in my ear. "How are you feeling?"

"I'm okay." I looked at him, his kind eyes and sweet smile. His concern for me was real. In that moment, I wanted to kiss him. Maybe if his mom wasn't right behind us, in the kitchen. Maybe, if I knew for sure he wanted to kiss me too. How could I have been thinking of kissing anyway?

Joan's voice pulled me from my thoughts. "Dinner's ready. Ian, come make the drinks. Lola, we have water, tea, and lemonade. What would you like?"

I followed Ian back into the kitchen. "Water is fine, thank you."

"Lola, sit here!" Sammy pointed to the empty chair next to his and I sat down.

Joan walked over with a bowl full of pasta in her hands and surveyed the table. "Looks like we're out of room. I'll just pass this around and put it back over there when we're done."

"So, Mom, you done any past-life regressions lately?" Ian

said as he scooped a mountain of spaghetti onto his plate and then mine.

Joan looked at me, a smidge of panic flashed in her eyes.

"Don't worry about Lola. She's cool with reincarnation. In fact, I was hoping you'd tell her more about it."

She took the pasta bowl. "Is this an interest of yours, Lola?" She helped herself to a less hearty portion and then returned the nearly empty bowl to the counter.

"Umm, well, Ian has been telling me a bit about the subject." I looked in his direction, feeling my face get hot.

"Yeah, I think Lola has been flashing back to a past life," Ian blurted. I nearly choked on the bite of spaghetti I'd just taken. Why was he telling her already? Why was he telling her at all?

Joan looked in my eyes as if to get a better read on the situation. "Do you want to tell me about it?"

"It's really nothing."

"Nothing?!?" Ian said, irritation in his voice. "You passed out and woke up on a train to Auschwitz. You call that nothing?"

I pushed a meatball around on my plate and remained silent.

"Son, the idea of reincarnation doesn't sit with everyone. You have to be respectful of what others believe and, clearly, the subject is making her uncomfortable."

"Lola, tell her the story," Ian urged. "It makes all the sense in the world. It's a clear-cut case."

I thought about my dad and Zandria. I thought about Mom, lying in bed, zombie-like, with those sleeping pills on the table next to her. I thought of the way everything seemed to be changing and not in the direction of normal. I knew that the only life that mattered was this one.

"Unless it has anything to do with this life now, I don't want to think about it." I felt the tears burning my eyes. "Excuse me." I rushed from the table and to the bathroom.

Standing in front of the mirror, I watched my eyes overflow

with tears. A hopeless feeling washed over me.

There was a gentle knock. "Lola, I'm sorry," Ian said.

I wiped my eyes, straightened my spine and opened the door. "I'm ready to go home. Can you take me home?"

Chapter 9

"I'm leaving for the airport now." Dad tugged on my foot through the quilt. I forced my eyes open to see him sitting on the edge of the bed. His normally tired eyes were now clear and alive.

"Okay." I rolled over. We'd barely talked since Saturday. I couldn't exactly be normal now. I still loved him, but I hated what he was doing.

"Keep an eye on your mother for me."

"What do you think I've been doing all summer?"

Dad laughed nervously. "Well, you're on overtime now. Try to stick close to home and watch how many pills she's taking."

"I've been doing all of that already. Just go on your trip." I felt like crying again. I didn't want him to go on the trip. I wanted to beg him to stay instead. But he wouldn't. He was happy about leaving us. These last few days, I'd pushed him farther away instead of bringing him closer. I'm sure he wanted to go more than ever now.

He placed a heavy hand on my leg. "I love you."

"Mhmmm." I couldn't say it back.

He waited for a moment before rising from the bed. I didn't need to look at him to see the disappointment on his face.

Hours later, I woke with the sun beaming through the curtains. I didn't want to get out of bed, but more than that, I didn't want to be like Mom. I got up and trudged my way to the bathroom. The house was completely silent. I peeked in Dad's office at the clock. It read eleven o'clock. I'd slept through breakfast and so had Mom. I went downstairs to check on her. The room was dark, the blackout shades were doing their job. I shook Mom's shoulder gently. She didn't move or make a sound. I inspected the pill bottle. At least three pills gone since yesterday. She must have had some spell of insomnia last night to take that many. This was really getting worse. I needed to find a way to get her back to the doctor or at least get her to take the right pills, the ones that help. I hadn't encouraged her much the last couple of days. I'd been obsessed with Dad's online girlfriend.

Just the night before, I'd joined Twitter under a fake name and watched ZanyZandria's tweets. I wanted to catch her talking to or about Dad. She didn't mention NickRay68, though. She talked about her obnoxious dog and how she wished her ex would take him on the weeks he takes the kids. She posted a picture of her dinner for one, a cheesy salmon concoction and promised the recipe to a few of her "tweeps." But there was no mention of the coming romantic encounter with my father. No mention of the family she was breaking up.

I left Mom for the kitchen where I put on a fresh pot of coffee in the hopes that she'd soon come out of her cave. I breathed in the scent of the coffee and meditated on the gurgling sound coming from the machine, a small way to force peace upon myself.

I was halfway up the steps when the phone rang. I flung myself across the bed, grabbing it on the fourth ring, right before the answering machine. I was the only kid my age that still relied on the family landline as a method of communication. Mom was ridiculous when it came to cell phones. She only had one of her own because Dad made her.

"Hello, my name is Biff Billings from the sociology department at TAU. We have been studying cheerleaders in their natural habitat and have been made aware that there seems to be a rare breed of one in your household. Our records indicate that this cheerleader prefers books to shiny objects. It would be delightful if we could meet this specimen face-to-face as it is such a rarity to find one of these creatures that actually has a brain."

"Ha ha, Ian. You're so funny. Would you like me to Google the nearest comedy club so you can go and audition?"

"I'm sorry, no. I just can't pull myself away from this research. TAU needs my brilliant mind," he said, not breaking from character.

"Well, Mr. Billings, or should I say Dr.? What is TAU anyway?"

"You mean you haven't heard of us? Totally Awesome University? We were voted biggest party school and best-looking student body two years in a row. How could you not know about us?"

Instead of coming up with a witty response, I laughed. Hard. It wasn't even that funny, but I couldn't stop laughing.

"Lola? You gonna make it over there? It sounds like you're convulsing," Ian said from the other end of the line.

"Thank you," I said when I finally regained my composure.

"For what, being a jackass?"

"That and saving me from myself."

"Did I interrupt your suicide plunge?"

"Only if it'd kill me to spend the day waiting for my father's mistress to tweet about their get-together." I held the phone up with my shoulder and reached across the nightstand for my laptop.

"He left this morning, huh?"

"Yep." I opened the screen and started to type.

"What is that noise? Lola, is that typing I hear?" Ian asked. "Close the screen and back away from the device. I'm coming to get you right now!"

I laughed again. "I can't go anywhere. I gotta watch Mom."

"Well, I'm still coming to you. I'll be there in fifteen minutes. Until then stay off the computer." The line clicked and he was gone.

I looked at the screen. www.twi was typed in the box. I put my fingers back on the keys and finished typing. The page came up, but her name was not there. I started to type it into the search box. Instead, I hit the X. If Ian was coming in fifteen minutes, I needed to get ready.

I put on a pair of cutoffs and my Washington High Cheerleader t-shirt—the one they gave me when I made the squad—just to make Ian laugh. I pulled my hair back into a ponytail and went to check on Mom. The coffee was ready, but she wasn't.

"Mom, it's late. Wake up!" I shook her gently at first and then harder.

"God, Nick, leave me the hell alone." She slapped my arm away and rolled over.

I walked to the window and pulled up the shade. She yanked the covers over her head. I went into the kitchen and poured her a cup of coffee with half-n-half, like she likes it. I remembered how she used to load it with sugar and wished she could give up depression as easily.

"Here's your coffee, Mom." I spoke to her as if she was ninety-years-old and hard-of-hearing. "What channel do you want to watch?" I picked up the remote and flipped to The Food Network.

She rubbed her hand across the empty space next to her in bed before sitting up. She took in the room, confusion pasted on her face. "Where's your father? What time is it?"

"He left for Austin this morning. It's eleven-thirty."

"Austin?"

"Business trip, remember?"

She nodded in agreement, but I could tell she didn't remember. "Here." I handed her the coffee. "Would you like something to eat?"

"I'm not hungry," she mumbled.

I left the room and came back with an apple and a banana. "Here's something, in case you get hungry," I said as the doorbell rang. "That's Ian. I'll check on you in a bit."

"Who's Ian?"

"Our neighbor . . . my friend." I gave her the answer but she just stared at the TV. I guess I should be grateful she even asked.

I opened the front door and of course Ian's eyes settled on my shirt. "Ah, yes, we are at the right place. Let me just go get my team and the equipment." He turned his back to me and I yanked him through the doorway.

"How'd you get away today? Shouldn't you be home with Sammy?"

"Nah, he went to the zoo with a buddy in our other neighborhood. I got nothing on the agenda today except saving cheerleaders."

"Well, normally, I'm quite fond of my independence, but I guess I could use the company." I sat down on the couch and Ian did the same.

"Independence, I see." Ian nodded. I think he'd finally realized I wasn't exaggerating that night. Despite Hannah and the cheerleading squad, he was the closest thing to a *real* friend that I had.

"What's new?" I asked, breaking the silence.

"I don't know. You tell me. You were the one who promised to call but didn't."

"I didn't know what to say after I made you take me home early. I felt stupid." I twisted the end of the t-shirt around my fingers, counting the beats of Ian's tapping foot. "Can we just pretend it never happened?"

"It wasn't stupid and I promise not to bring it up again." He made an imaginary X across his chest with his finger. "Now, tell me about your dad."

"Hold on." I got up and looked in the kitchen then returned to the couch. "I just wanted to make sure Mom hasn't crept out of bed. The last thing she needs is to hear any of this."

"So, did you make any new discoveries?"

"I joined Twitter."

"You didn't?"

"I did. I'm a glutton for punishment."

"No, you're just a nosy little brat." Ian reached out and patted my thigh with a smile on his face. My stomach flipped. "So did you learn anything?"

"Just that she hates her dog and isn't a vegetarian."

"Maybe he isn't going to see her after all?"

"Why don't we go see?" I got up and made a run for the stairs. Ian ran after me. Just as I reached for the computer on the nightstand, Ian threw his arm across my back and pulled me down.

"Do not get that computer!" He was winded from the sprint to my room. We laid across the bed on our stomachs, side by side, laughing and trying to catch our breath at the same time. In one simultaneous movement, we both took a deep breath and rolled over on our backs, staring at the ceiling like it was the star-filled sky.

"I'm scared," I said and then started to sob. And again as if we choreographed this dance, we rolled toward each other. Ian's chin rested on the top of my head, his arms around me. I held my hands together in praying position as my tears poured onto his chest.

By the time I finished crying, I felt like I'd completed a marathon and Ian hadn't moved a muscle. I looked up at him. "Thank you."

"No problemo. That's what friends are for, right?"

"If so, I guess Hannah missed the memo." I sat up. Ian's arm slipped away.

He sat up next to me. "Well, I don't know about Hannah, but I really do care about you, Lola." He looked into my eyes and there was a hint of something more. It made me nervous, in a good way. He reached for my hand, but instead of letting him take it, I got up and grabbed the laptop. As much as I liked him, I didn't want anything between us to get weird.

"Don't you at least want to meet her?" I raised my eyebrow at him as I opened the computer. "Holy crap, she changed her avatar. And I know her. I know I know her from somewhere. She looks so familiar."

Ian kneeled behind me on the floor, staring over my shoulder at the screen. "Somehow I was expecting someone much hotter."

"She did have the Texas Longhorns symbol here. I got a glimpse of a picture of her one day, but this is the first time I'm really seeing her. I think it's her eyes. There is something about them."

Ian took the computer and clicked a few times. I watched him as he read, waiting for him to tell me what he learned. He didn't speak, but his smile quickly faded. He closed the computer. "Well, nothing interesting there. What say we go back downstairs?"

I started to ask, but was interrupted by a crash from downstairs. "LOLA!" Mom's voice boomed.

Ian and I hustled down the steps, but I ran by myself into the kitchen. The coffee pot was shattered on the floor and coffee was splattered across the cabinets. "What happened?"

"Damn it, I can't get my hands to stop shaking long enough to pour myself a cup of coffee."

"So you threw it?"

"I didn't mean to." She slid against the cabinets to the floor, burying her face in her knees. I remembered what Ian did for me only minutes ago. I walked to her side and put my arms around her. She sobbed and shook and I finally understood.

When she had no tears left to cry, she stood up and walked to the table. "I think I'd like to eat now."

"Bagel?" I asked as I stepped carefully around the broken glass and opened the pantry.

"Do we have any walnut cream cheese?"

"Dad stocked the fridge before he left." I put the bagel in the toaster and grabbed the cream cheese from the fridge in a rush to start cleaning up the mess.

Mom looked down at me sopping coffee up with a paper towel. "That was driving you crazy, wasn't it?"

"A little." I laughed while holding a stack of broken glass. "We're gonna need to go shopping now, you know?"

"You mean to tell me I'll have to put on clothes and brush my hair?" Mom smiled at the sound of her own joke and, suddenly, I remembered Ian.

I tossed the glass into the trash and stepped into the living room. He was not there. As I moved toward the stairs, I noticed a note, precariously placed on the doorknob.

You two need some time. I'll call you later. -E

Chapter 10

"Thank you, Lola, for getting me out of the house." Mom turned on the lights as we walked through the door, back from our impromptu shopping trip.

"You're the one who set the ball in motion. How would you survive tomorrow without coffee?" I put the shopping bags on the table and eased the coffee pot out of one of them. "Now if we can figure this thing out."

Mom stepped around the kitchen table and to the doorway of her dark bedroom, kicked her flip flops off and then sat down across from me. I tossed her the instruction booklet and pulled the machine out of the box. The new one wasn't very different from the other one, but I stretched out that time with her as long as I could. I went over to the counter and picked up the old machine. "What do I do with this one? Throw it away?"

"Oh, my God." Mom's head dropped into her hands and she started to shake. I put the machine down and rushed over to her. Before I could say a word I realized she was laughing, not crying. I looked at the booklet in her hand. There was a picture of the machine and a separate picture of the carafe. The epiphany—that we should have only replaced the broken carafe—and the laughter struck me too. I think we laughed longer than either of us had cried earlier in the day.

"Want to take it back and just get the part we need?" I asked when the wave of laughter ended. "Store's still open for another two hours."

"Nah, I like this new one better."

"They're basically the same coffeemaker."

"No way. The button sticks on the old one. It's not possible this one has that feature." Mom carried the new machine to the counter and plugged it in.

"Want to watch a movie?" I asked.

"Only if we watch it in the bedroom. I'm exhausted." Mom stretched her hands toward the ceiling and shuffled to her room.

"I'll just put on my PJ's and meet you back here," I said from the doorway as she moved through her bedroom to her bathroom. I couldn't help but notice the pill bottle was no longer on the nightstand. I guess as exhausted as she was, it wasn't enough to get her to sleep.

Upstairs, I changed clothes and brushed my teeth. I realized that today Mom had helped me get my mind off my problems with Dad the way he used to help me get my mind off the problems with her. I wished he wasn't so different this time, so distracted. I decided to give him a call. Maybe I could apologize and that would be enough to keep him from seeing Zandria.

"You've reached Nick Ray Designs. Leave your name and number and I'll get back to you."

"Hey, Dad. Haven't heard from you yet. I hope you made it safely to the Lone Star state. I'm sorry for everything lately. I hope that when you get back, we can just go back to normal. I love you." I started to hang up, but remembered one more thing. "Oh yeah, also thought you'd want to know that Mom and I went out this evening. Shopping and dinner. We're getting ready to watch a movie, too. Call me later. Bye."

I made it to the kitchen when the phone rang. It was Dad.

"Hey, Lola. I just missed you. I'm sorry I didn't call. It's been a crazy day."

"I imagine," I said. "Did you get the message I left?"

"Not yet, just saw the missed call. Figured it was you. I was in the shower, cleaning up and settling in before I gave you a ring."

"Well, Mom and I are good. She got up. We went out."

"That's great, really."

"You want to talk to her?" I walked into her room. She was already in bed.

"Well, I, uhm, I really just wanted to check in. I've got to work on my presentation for tomorrow. But if she's right there, I suppose." His voice trailed off and I realized Mom was already asleep.

"It's okay, Dad. Go work on your stuff."

"I love you, Lola."

"You, too. Talk to you later." I put down the phone and climbed into the king-size bed next to Mom. The TV was already on so I grabbed the remote and raised the volume. I was going to watch a movie with my mother whether she was an active participant or not. I sat frozen against the headboard, too out of it to even bother with a pillow. I had no tears left, no energy for an emotional outburst of any kind. I was just still, with pictures swirling in my head. Mom, Dad, our happy family, our manic family, our sad family, Zandria, me, a house without my father, the train, those eyes. And then I heard it, the train, more specifically the squealing sound of its brakes. I closed my eyes.

The crowded train car is hot and it smells—urine, feces, sickness, decaying flesh. The bodies around me are limp. I hear

moaning and soft whimpering but little else. My breathing is shallow. I am thirsty. I am hungry. On either side of me are my parents, their hands in mine, though neither of them seems to be conscious of this. Mother's eyes are closed. Father's are wide open. He barely blinks. His lips are dry. So are mine.

The train slows. The rumble of the tracks beneath us changes. A new sound, squealing brakes, the massive machine being forced to a halt. Soon there is no more rumble at all. Silence. We have arrived at our destination. The men, women, and children move slowly to their feet. The Stars of David rise and wait. It's only seconds before the doors slide open, but it feels much longer. Light rushes into our boxcar and the voice of a soldier calls our attention. I look his way and all I see are his piercing blue eyes.

"No, Nick, no. Don't leave!" My mom cried out.

And just like that, I was back in bed. Mom was lying next to me, talking in her sleep. I wondered if she had some sort of sixth sense. Had her dreams transported her to Austin? Was Dad on his way out with Zandria?

I went upstairs to get my computer. I was back on the website reading the thoughts of ZanyZandria in one hundred and forty characters or less. I found the tweet, the one Ian attempted to hide from me. *Looking forward to a face-to-face meet with a really special online friend.*

I clicked on the small picture of her. Once enlarged I was drawn to her eyes. They were the same piercing blue as the soldier's in my dream. I picked up the phone and dialed Ian's number.

"I did it again," I said when he answered the phone.

"Did what?"

"Flashed back. I was on the train. It reached the stop. The doors opened and there was this man. He's someone in this life, I know it."

"Was it another dream? Is everything okay? Are you stressed again?" Ian sounded worried.

"I guess I fell asleep, but I swear I heard the train brakes while I was still awake. Mom and I were supposed to watch a movie, but she took some pills and crashed. Maybe that was enough stress to send me back."

"So, who do you think the man is?"

"Well, he was a soldier and he had these blue eyes. I'm not positive, but I think I'm looking at those eyes right now on Twitter." I held the phone while staring at the computer screen.

"Are you stalking her page again?"

"Yes, but only to see if I'm right about those eyes. And I am. If I saw a picture of the soldier, I'd ask if he was ZanyZandria's brother. Is it possible? Could she have been a he back then?"

"I think our souls have a gender preference. But we also live lots of lives and I'm sure we switch teams sometimes. Who knows, I could have been a girl before."

"It's her then. I'm sure of it."

"I don't know. I think you need to get the whole picture to be that sure."

"And how do you suppose I do that? Work myself into a full-blown panic attack in order to collect information? I don't think so."

"You don't have to do that. I'll hypnotize you!"

"Now you're really a comedian!" I laughed.

"No, I've been researching it and I've found a couple of scripts that should work. People pay my mom to do this for them. It works and it heals people."

"How's it going to heal me? All I want is for my mom to get better and my dad to stay with us, so we can be a normal family. Will going back do that?" My heart pounded.

"I don't know. It could. I think you need to go back and see what it's trying to show you."

"What do you mean I need to?" I finally closed the screen and pushed the laptop away.

"Most people go through their whole lives without ever considering that they've been here before. It's simply not something they need to know. Mom always says that if a memory from the past comes up, it needs to be dealt with."

"This isn't a memory from my past though." I twisted my hair. "And what am I supposed to deal with anyway?"

"I feel certain it is your past. And what you need to deal with will be shown to you. And the fact that you met me, and that my mom does what she does, just proves that I'm here to help you." Ian got quiet for a moment. "There are no coincidences, Lola."

"Why do you care so much about this past-life stuff?"

"When my mom first helped a patient uncover a past life, it not only changed the patient's life, but it changed Mom's too. It was like this fire was lit inside of her. I admired it," his voice cracked. "Mom threw herself into her work and that was the beginning of the end of her and Dad's marriage. But she was alive like I'd never seen her. I started studying the books she left lying around. The stuff's fascinating and it keeps me close to her."

"How did you get to be such a good guy?"

"Minimal exposure to assholes, I guess." Ian paused on the other end. "Now what do you say to the hypnosis?"

"If I say yes, what does that entail?"

"Trusting me."

"I do trust you."

"Good," Ian said and I was convinced I heard his smile.

"So, tomorrow?"

"Okay."

"It's a date then . . . or should I say appointment?"

"Ian White, I think you have your first hypnotherapy client," I laughed.

"Thank you, Lola. Goodnight now."

"Night." I hung up the phone and reached for a book instead of my computer. For now, I didn't need to know what Zandria was up to.

Chapter 11

"I'm here," Ian called me on his cell from his truck in our driveway a little after one o'clock. He'd just gotten back from Joan's house. I was in the living room with Mom while she watched that show about pregnant teenagers. Resisting the urge to get sucked in to bad reality TV, I tried to read the book Ian gave me about past-life regressions. She didn't bother to ask me what I was reading. I guess it had taken all of her energy just to be out of bed and on the couch. I should have been grateful for that, instead of longing for her interest.

I made it to the door before Ian did and stepped outside. I didn't really want him to see my zombie-mom.

"I snagged this from Mom's office, relaxation music." He held out a CD as he approached the front step. "Where do you want to do this?"

"I don't know." I nodded my head toward the house. "She's out of bed today."

"That's great. Two days in a row, huh?"

"Yes, but I'm not sure how that works with our hypnotherapy session."

"Let's go to the old man's place then." Ian turned toward his second home across the street.

I opened the door and leaned inside. "Mom, will you be okay for a few hours?"

"Are you going somewhere?" She turned her head in my direction, but kept her eyes on the TV.

"Just to Ian's house."

"Across the street?"

"Yes, Mom."

"I'll be fine then. You go. I'm glad you have a friend." Mom lifted the remote control off the table and increased the volume. I held onto her last words for a moment. Was it really that big a deal that Ian and I were friends?

I closed the door and skipped across the yard to catch up with Ian. "Should I move the truck?" He asked as he threw his leg up sideways and kicked me.

"Nah, it'll be fine." I hip-checked him.

When we got to the front door, Ian fiddled with the keys. His long slim fingers were dotted with a few freckles and his hands shook a little. I wondered if this was a quirk I'd yet to notice or was he nervous? If so, was it because of the hypnotism or me?

"You go pick the comfiest chair and I'll get my dad's CD player," he said once the door was open and we were inside.

I walked to the living room and tried out a few seats. I settled on the burgundy leather recliner. I pulled the handle on the side and watched my feet rise. The chair was comfortable. Closing my eyes, I leaned my head back.

"I see you're all ready." Ian placed the portable CD player on the table and stretched the cord to the nearest outlet.

"Do you need me to move?" I asked.

"Nope, I need you to be comfy and cozy, so stay right where you are."

Ian started the music. It was gentle and enchanting, with soft bells and a harp, maybe. I was scared and excited. The scenes I'd visited so far were just awful and whatever was going to happen there couldn't be good. But Ian was so into all of this, I loved seeing this side of him. And if I was opening up to this past-life stuff and was willing to accept I was that girl on the train, maybe I did want to know what happened to her . . . or me.

Ian's voice broke through my thoughts, taking on a very serious tone. "You see a stairway leading down. You are going to follow this path, going down, down, down, deeper, and deeper." I relaxed in the chair. It was amazing how the words soothed me. He really did have a voice for this kind of thing. I could see the stairs clearly in my mind. I followed the directions, feeling lighter with every step.

He continued, "At the end of the stairs, there is a doorway. The doorway leads to a garden. Walk through the doorway and look around." I could hardly feel the chair anymore. I wandered through the garden, passing rose bushes of all colors. Red, white, yellow, and even black. I stared at the black roses. They seemed wrong, ominous, a sign of things to come. I walked away from them, focused instead at the beauty all around.

Ian's voice sounded again, as if from an overhead speaker. I wasn't in the chair at all anymore. It really felt that I was walking through the garden. "In this garden, you will see a mirror. Go to the mirror and stand in front of it."

I found the mirror and looked into it. Ian spoke again, "I will count backwards from ten. By the time I get to one, the mirror will become a door to the past. Ten, nine, eight, seven . . ."

I'm on the train. The mirror is now the doorway, the exit from this cage we've dwelled in for days. The soldier stands before us, a large dog, a shepherd, at his side.

"Move, you filthy, vile creatures!" He screams as he pulls a

woman off the train by her hair. He throws her to one side. As we move closer, I realize all the men are being pushed to one side, all the women and children to the other. I clutch my father's hand tighter than before. I notice a tear tumble out from Mother's eye. A little girl behind me starts to whine. Her voice is quickly muffled. The soldier grabs my father by the arm and pulls him off the train. Papa does not let go of my hand and soon Mother and I are lying on top of him on the ground. We have all fallen down because our desire to stay connected is more powerful than the reaction to keep our balance and stay on two feet.

The soldier draws his gun. He points it at Mother. "Get up! Get up all of you! Now!"

We scramble to our feet. He rips my father's hand from mine. "NO!" I scream and throw my arms around Papa's waist. Then I feel the cold metal against my forehead. My father pries my hands off of him, pushes me away. I am on the ground on my knees. I look up and see the gun. To my left, my mother weeps. To my right, my father moves slowly away from us. He looks over his shoulder and into my eyes. The soldier cocks the gun. I look up into his piercing blue eyes. I will never forget them.

"Get up and go with the women." The soldier uses his gun, the one that had been aimed at my face, to point me in the direction I need to go. I rush to Mother's side. We huddle together, crying. The soldier leaves us and walks toward Papa. "You filthy bastard!" He says and pushes Papa into the line with the other men. I go limp in Mother's arms. Papa is gone.

"Lola, wake up. Wake up, please. You're scaring me." Ian shook me. My body trembled and my face was wet with tears.

"Oh, my God," I cried.

"What the hell happened to you? You were out of it, somewhere else, totally losing it." Ian paced back and forth in front of the chair.

"I believe you now. I was there. I lived it. And I know who Zandria is," I whispered.

Ian sat down on the couch in front of me. "You do?"

"She's the soldier that took my dad—from that life—away when we got off the train." I tugged at the lever on the chair and put my feet back on the floor. "Can I get a drink of water? My throat hurts."

Ian jumped up and ran to the kitchen. He was out in seconds carrying a glass of water. It spilled a little as he handed it to me. Even he was trembling. He sat down in front of me and I watched him silently. His eyes were filled with fascination. I could see the wheels spinning in his head, but he couldn't seem to choose the question he wanted to start with.

"You did it," I said.

"I know. I can't believe it worked. You should have seen it, Lo. You were there."

"Uh, yeah. I think I know that." I shook my head. "But why me? That shouldn't have been that easy."

"Like I said before, I guess you needed the information."

"Great. Now I know that Zandria broke up my family before. So what? That means it's supposed to hurt less when she does it this time?" I gulped down the water. "Am I supposed to stop her?"

"Maybe."

"Maybe to which part?"

"Both."

I hopped up from the chair and headed toward the door.

"Where are you going?" Ian called after me. "You need to sit here and rest a while longer."

"I need to go find Zandria." I opened the door and ran across the street. When I got inside, Mom was no longer on the couch. I wanted to ignore her and run straight upstairs, but I didn't. I walked to her bedroom and stepped inside. The curtains were drawn. It was dark and quiet and smelled subtly of coffee. She was in bed, asleep.

Upstairs in my room, I logged onto Twitter. Conveniently enough, @zanyZandria had followed me back and, because of that, I could send her a private message. I clicked through to send her a direct message and saw the empty box before my eyes on the screen. How do I put this into words?

Hi, this is Nick's daughter.I know you 2 r friends.I don't want him 2 leave us.

I started to hit send, but changed my mind. I couldn't confront her. If I was shown the vision to stop her from pursuing my dad and breaking up our family again, then I guessed I'd just failed. I pushed the computer aside and walked to the window. Ian's truck was still in our driveway. I picked up the phone and dialed his number.

"You okay?" he asked instead of saying hello.

"I don't know. I just wrote her a direct message."

"You did what?"

"It said I knew about them and I didn't want Dad to leave us. I didn't send it though. Lost my nerve." I walked over to the closet and pulled out the vacuum, hoping the lines would make me better.

"Well, that's a relief."

"You think?"

"You don't want to out yourself. It's not your stuff."

"How is it not my stuff? He's my father!" I paused for a second to think. "I thought you said I was shown the vision so I could stop it from happening again."

"That's one explanation, sure. But I don't think you do it by talking to her. You don't even know anything about her." He paused. "Can I come over?"

I made Ian leave before dinner. He fought to stay, but truthfully, I just didn't want him there when Mom came out of her cave. I didn't think I could handle the awkward silence that was likely to hover over the room. And, of course, knowing Ian, he'd try to break it with a joke that Mom was in no state of mind to find funny. I put a pot of water on the stove for spaghetti and ran upstairs to check Twitter.

There it was. A new post to my dad.

Wishing @nickray68 safe travels. Don't give up, remember what I told you.

What does that mean? I wondered if she had some sort of plan to get him into her life for good. Maybe Dad had doubts about it working. What did she tell him?

"LOLA!" Mom called from downstairs. "This pot of water is boiling over. Come do something about it!"

Do it yourself! I thought as I got up from the computer and walked downstairs.

Chapter 12

Dad's voice woke me up. "Hello! Anybody here?" He walked up the steps. "It's eleven o'clock in the morning. Are you guys really still sleeping?" He knocked gently on my bedroom door.

"Come in," I answered. I could feel the anxiety blossoming in my gut. Would he look different, act different now?

He stopped at the foot of my bed. I studied his eyes, looking for a hint that something or someone had changed him. "How were things while I was away?" he asked.

"Fine, I guess."

"And your mother got out of bed?"

"For a little while."

"Did you get out and have some fun?"

"Went to Ian's."

"You guys are getting close, huh?" He took a seat at the end of the bed.

"He's funny." I sat up cross-legged under the covers. "And smart."

"Anything I should concern myself with? Do I need to put a lock on the outside of this door?" Dad laughed. I didn't. I wasn't really looking for a light-hearted father-daughter moment.

"It's not like that. We're just friends." I cleared my throat ready to go out on a limb and ask about Zandria. "How was Texas?" I chickened out.

"It was good. Made some major progress with the clients, ate some incredible barbeque, and cleared my mind a little."

"Cleared your mind?"

"I'm sorry I've been so checked out, Lola. I want to do better. Really." He reached over and placed his hand on mine.

"Have you seen Mom yet?"

"Not yet." He stood up and walked to the bedroom door. "I'll go downstairs and check on her."

I lay back down and counted the thuds as he made his way down the steps. I heard the hesitation in his movement. I climbed out of bed and surveyed my room. I stared at the path Dad's feet created on the carpet and decided not to vacuum.

Downstairs, I tiptoed into the kitchen and listened for voices from their bedroom. I peeked through the doorway as I walked by and saw that Dad had lifted the shades to let some light in. He opened and closed drawers, but didn't talk. Mom was quiet too, which I could only assume meant that her sleep was too deep to be disturbed by Dad's presence.

"Don't you want to tell her you're home?" I asked as he joined me in the kitchen. He reached into the cabinet for a mug. I noticed the confused look on his face as he poured the coffee. "The coffee pot's new," I added.

"Dare I even ask?" He pulled out the chair in front of me at the table and reached over for the milk.

"It's a long story. And you didn't answer my question. Are you going to wake her or not?"

"I tried. She's out like a light."

"Try harder."

"Seeing her like that just throws me back into the exhaustion of it all." His head fell to his hand and he rubbed his brow. "I'm tired of having to save her."

"But you haven't even tried this time. You've left it all to me while you escape into your work . . . or whatever you're escaping to." I dropped my spoon into the cereal bowl.

"I'm sorry about that, Lola." Dad got up and pushed his chair in. "I'm desperate for some normalcy."

"You're not the only one," I mumbled as Dad walked out of the room.

I wasn't hungry anymore. I pushed the half-eaten bowl of cereal away and gazed around the room. The silence was unbearable. I wanted to go back in time to some busy morning before school. I wanted to hear Mom humming as she poured her coffee and see Dad stretching as he walked through the bedroom door, claiming that we had woken him up with our noise. Then he'd ask her to fry him up some bacon and she'd make a snide remark about his fat ass. They wouldn't be a perfect couple, but they'd perhaps be a normal couple.

I got up and poured some coffee for Mom. I walked into her bedroom and set the cup down on the night table. I opened the bottle of sleeping pills and dumped them into my hands. *One, two, three, four, five . . .*

"You checking up on me?" Mom's voice was low and raspy.

"I, uh, just, uh, wanted to make sure." I put the pills back into the bottle and screwed on the cap.

"It's okay. I'd check on me too, if I were you." Mom took the bottle from my hand and stared at it. "I wake up in the middle of the night and you can't imagine the things that go through my head. I'm so scared, Lola."

"What are you scared of, Mom?"

"I don't know. Everything and nothing. This world is so cruel and unjust. I have this nightmare of you and your father being ripped away from me. It's so irrational, but it haunts me. You go away and I'm left with only insanity. I'm a madwoman, Lola."

I understood her nightmare. I wanted to tell her I'd seen it, but didn't want to send her further into her fear. "Did you talk to Dad this morning?"

"He's home?" She sat up and grabbed the clock. "Is it Friday already?"

"He got home about an hour ago. Said he tried to wake you."

She rolled over and started crying. "I hate this. I hate who I am!"

I crawled under the covers and wrapped my arms around her. "Why don't we go to the doctor?"

She nodded. I kept my arms around her until she sat up and wiped her cheek.

Her eyes glazed over. "I'm going to shower now."

When the sound of the water filled the room, I ran upstairs.

"Dad, Dad!" I called as I burst into his office. He was on the couch, his eyes fixed on a spot on the ceiling.

"What's going on?" He jumped up.

"Mom agreed to go to the doctor. Will you make the call?"

"Are you sure?"

"She's in the shower right now. She's getting ready to go." I ran to Dad's desk and shuffled through the rolodex. The fact that the doctor's number resided in that ancient device was proof of how long he'd been an integral part of our lives. "Here, call him!"

Dad hesitated to take the phone from my hand. I dialed and shoved it toward him.

"Hi, yes, I was calling to see if it was possible to get Christine Ray in to see Dr. Koman today?" He paced as he waited for a response. "Okay. Thank you."

"And?" I said as he hung up the phone.

"She has an appointment at three o'clock.

I resisted the urge to jump up and down, but gave Dad a big hug. If the doctor could help Mom pull it together, maybe Dad wouldn't leave after all. I went to my room and looked for something to wear. The phone rang as I was deciding between capri pants or a skirt.

"Hey, girl! I haven't heard from you or seen you on Facebook in like forever. Where have you been?" Hannah's voice blared from the other end.

"I thought you were at the beach," I replied.

"I am, but I got a better phone a couple of weeks ago, so I'm always on Facebook. All you have to do is message me."

"Yeah, I haven't checked Facebook in a while."

"What the hell have you been doing then?" Hannah snapped.

"Just hanging out."

"Oh, Lord, please don't tell me you've been hanging out with the freak!"

How is it that was her first guess? And why couldn't she call Ian by his name? Hearing her call him a freak made me cringe. "Why do you assume that, Hannah?"

"Well, let's see. It's summer and you can't drive, so chances are you aren't leaving the house too often. I keep up with everyone and no one's told me they've seen you, so who else could you be hanging with?"

"I'm spending a lot of time with my mom." My voice broke as I answered.

"So, she's okay this summer?"

"Yep, she's doing great. I've been going with her to the studio and making collages."

"You know, for the sake of your reputation, you really should consider giving Bethanie a call."

"I've only said two words to her in my life."

"Well, when you get to cheerleading camp you better change that. We have to get invited to her back-to-school party."

"Whatever, Hannah. Listen, I really need to get ready. We're going to, uh, the mall in about an hour."

"All right, chica! Have fun and stay away from freaks! Later." Hannah hung up as I contemplated the lies I'd just told. Why did it matter what Hannah thought anyway?

There was a knock at my bedroom door just as I pulled the dress over my head. "Hold on!" I yelled. I buttoned up the front and opened the door.

"Your mother is back in bed," Dad said.

"What?" I pushed past him and ran down the stairs. When I got to their bedroom door, I could see he was right. "Mom! What are you doing?"

"That shower took it out of me, Lola. I'm just so weak."

"Dad made you an appointment with Dr. Koman at three."

"Why did he do that?" Her face got red. "Bastard."

"It's not his fault Mom. I told him to."

"Why? What on earth were you thinking?" she shouted.

"I asked you if you would go to the doctor and you said yes. You told me you were scared and wanted help."

"I did no such thing, Lola."

"But you told me—"

Mom interrupted, "I confided in you as a friend, not so you could come up with some grand scheme to save me."

"But you need help. I'm so tired of you staying in bed. I want my mom back." I lowered my head to hide the tears.

Mom shook her head. "That doctor will do nothing but poison me with his drugs and turn me into a damn zombie."

I lifted my head and looked into her eyes. "You already are a zombie. And someone has to get you to snap out of it!"

"Get out!" she hissed. "I can't believe you just destroyed my trust like that."

I ran out of her room. Dad stood outside the door. He'd heard everything. I went into the living room and picked up the remote control. I hoped Dad would go in and talk to Mom. In the old days, he would have. Instead he walked by me, carrying a new cup of coffee.

"Aren't you going to talk to her?" I asked through tears.

"No, I'm going to cancel the appointment and get back to work."

"What about Mom?"

"I was fooling myself thinking I could come back from this trip and change anything. I'm sick of this crap."

Chapter 13

Dad had been home from his trip for a week. He'd done little more than work and mope around the house. Mom made it to the couch in the living room a few times. In years past, Dad would celebrate those occasions the way a parent might dance a jig or sing a silly song when their baby finally walks. I needed to figure out how to encourage Mom on my own. It was beginning to sink in that this would be my burden to bear without any help from Dad. But, at least I had Ian. Life was more bearable with him across the street. It was his week at his Dad's, so I decided to call him.

"How are things feeling in your house right now?" I asked when he answered.

"Sammy's mesmerized by the Ninja hamsters, so I'd say we got peace like a river over here."

"Mind if I join you? I got tension you can cut with a knife over here."

"Your parents still aren't talking?" Ian asked.

"It's like waiting for a bomb to go off. I know it's going to happen, I just don't know when. So, can I come over?"

"Of course, you can!"

I put the phone down. "I'm going to Ian's," I yelled up to Dad from the bottom of the stairs. "I'll be back in a couple of hours."

"Check in on your mother before you go," Dad called back.

I ran through the kitchen and peeked into her bedroom. The TV blared, but not louder than her snoring. Nothing new.

In less than two minutes, I knocked on Ian's front door. "Come in," he yelled from inside. A battery-operated rat whipped across my path as I walked toward the kitchen.

"Hey, Lola!" Sammy shouted as he ran after the toy vermin.

"Nice rat, Sammy," I replied.

His face turned to a pout. "Hey, it's not a rat. It's a hamster."

"Sorry." I put my hands up in defense.

I walked into the kitchen to find Ian washing dishes. "A man after my own heart."

He looked at me, puzzled. "Huh?"

"It's a rare occasion that I come to this house and you aren't cleaning."

"Oh, yeah. Mom trained me well, I suppose. Must. Clean. House." Ian turned robotically in a circle.

"Oh, my gosh. You just reminded me. There is this cleaning website that I found when I was eleven," I grabbed a dish towel and started drying, "and I became absolutely obsessed with it. For an entire month, I wouldn't leave my room unless I was fully dressed, shoes and all, 'cause that's what the author of the website recommended. After I spilled a whole bottle of bleach trying to shine the sink, Mom blocked it from our computer."

"You are such a badass."

"I'm queen of the vacuum." I snapped the towel at him and laughed at my own joke. He didn't actually know how obsessed I was with vacuuming, but I wouldn't mind telling him someday.

"All finished!" Ian put the last dish in the drying rack and went to the living room. I hung the towel over the oven handle and followed him.

"So, what's new?" I asked when we were both sitting.

"You really want to talk about me?"

"Yes. We never talk about you."

"Let's see, last night I beat *Super Mario Galaxy* while Sammy cheered me on. This morning, I spent about two hours playing *Second Life* in between fishing the Ninja hamsters out from behind the furniture. And Dad just bought the entire series of *Battlestar Gallactica* on DVD, so we're totally going to have a Starbuck marathon over the next few days."

"You got any other video games?" I walked over to the entertainment center, eyeing the game selection.

"Lola, have you been holding out on me?"

"Well, as the story goes, back when my dad worked a corporate nine to five, he and I blew off steam playing video games. I was pretty darn good until my gaming partner went and became an entrepreneur." I looked over my shoulder, shooting Ian a mischievous look. I couldn't believe myself. But flirting with Ian did help get my mind off of things at home and the crazy flashbacks. Ian picked a game and fired up the Wii. We spent the next two hours glued to the controllers.

By the time I got home, little had changed. Mom was still in bed, though it appeared she had at least gotten up for coffee and lunch. I washed the dishes she'd left in the sink and swept the floor before going upstairs.

Dad was in his office with the door open. "Hey! You're home now?" he called from his desk.

I stopped at the doorway. "Yeah, I'm back."

"I could use a break. Why don't you come in and sit down." Dad nodded toward the couch.

I walked in slowly and sat down. "Twitter?" I said noticing the screen on his desk.

"Work Twitter, I'll have you know." I looked at the screen again. It was his business account.

I nodded. "So, was there something you wanted?"

"I just wanted to reconnect, I guess. Let you know I appreciate all that you're doing for your mom."

"I wish I didn't have to do it."

"I know. I can't believe she went off the meds." He grabbed the pen that was stuck behind his ear and started tapping it against his leg.

"Her giving the meds up has always been a possibility. I mean no one can force her. We're supposed to be prepared for this." I reached out and grabbed the pen. "You're supposed to be prepared for this."

"I wasn't." He leaned back in his desk chair.

"Why not? And don't say work."

"Then I got nothing to say." Dad spun around in his chair and began punching the keys on his computer. I got up and walked out.

In my room, I pulled the vacuum out and plugged it in. I took deep breaths and tried to focus on good memories as I ran it across the carpet. If I wanted to feel better about it, I could just say that vacuuming was my form of meditation. It was a weird habit though, and if people knew, they would think I was a freak. Even Ian would think I was a freak. Why in the world did I tell him I was queen of the vacuum? What the heck was I thinking?

I put the vacuum away and walked to the window. Sammy was bouncing a basketball in their driveway as Ian rolled circles on his skateboard in the road between our houses. I wished my life could be that simple. I wondered if this is how it felt for Ian when his parents' marriage was falling apart. Had he always been so cool about it all?

I lay down across the bed, careful not to wrinkle the quilt. I grabbed the book about past lives and flipped it open. After what

I'd seen in that hypnosis session of Ian's, I was a believer. Believing all this stuff seemed to make me more interesting in Ian's eyes. To everyone else, I'd seem just as crazy as my mom. Crazy. It was all so crazy.

I drifted back to the visions I'd had. The Holocaust. I'd actually been there. The silence of my room was interrupted by the sound of crying. It was muffled, far off. I told myself it was Sammy outside. He must have fallen off of Ian's skateboard. Yeah, that was it. I reached for my iPod, slipped the ear buds in, and closed my eyes, assuming the cries would go away.

My mother and I wait in a line of women. Guards march up and down, rifles draped over their shoulders, viscous dogs at their sides. Mother's hand is linked in mine. I can feel her trembling. I can feel us trembling. It is hard to decipher where she ends and I begin. We are instructed to strip. Voices erupt from the once-silent crowd. How can they ask this of us? They have sent us from our homes, torn us away from our fathers, husbands, and sons. Now they ask us to reveal all that we have that belongs just to us? A shot rings out, followed by a woman's blood-curdling scream. She refused to undress and now she is on the ground holding the lifeless, bleeding body of her baby in her arms. At the sight of this, my mother rips off her coat and pulls her shirt over her head. She urges me to do the same. I have never seen my mother undressed. Her large breasts fall upon her round stomach. Exposed like this, it is hard to tell I am her daughter. I am thin and flat in all the places where my mother is ample. I don't understand why this crosses my mind now, in this moment of nightmarish fear. The guards walk through the line, inspecting us. With the end of his rifle, he lifts one of mother's breasts. He releases a belly laugh as he pulls the metal away and her breast falls again to her stomach. He calls to the other

soldiers. Three of them stand before us now. He does it again. Three more times. Tears roll out of my mother's eyes and her hand grips mine tighter than ever. I close my eyes hard and scream at the top of my lungs. "STOP IT, NOW!" The rifle is off of my mother's breast and against my head.

"Lola."

I woke to the sound of knocking, relieved to be back in the present. I reached up and touched my head, where the gun had been. My hand throbbed as if someone was still gripping it.

"You mind helping me get dinner on the table?" Dad asked from the other side of the door.

I climbed out of bed, still trembling from the dream, and opened the door. "What are we having?"

"Baked chicken, broccoli, and mashed potatoes."

"What do you need me to do?" I leaned against the door frame to steady myself.

"Mash the potatoes."

I nodded and moved into the hall. "Is Mom eating with us?"

"I think so, she's in the shower." Dad followed me down the stairs.

In the kitchen, I reached under the cabinets and found the hand mixer. I strained the potatoes and dumped them into a bowl with butter, salt, and milk. As I stood at the counter mixing, I stared into the open doorway of my mother's bedroom. She emerged from the bathroom with only a towel wrapped around her hair. She had small breasts, a flat tummy, and legs that resembled stilts. She was nothing like the mom in my dream. I knew it was her, though. I wondered how we end up in new lives. What parts are decided by fate and what parts are decided by us? It was almost like Mom made a point to look completely different this time. But the essence—her essence—was still there.

Chapter 14

After dinner, I called Ian. "I was there again!"

"On the train or at the camp?" he asked.

"After the train, after my dad got taken away. Mom and I were in a line." I started to cry.

"Are you okay?"

"It was awful. They shot a baby. They humiliated my mother."

"How did it end?"

"Right before I woke up, they had a gun to my head." I paused to calm down. "I just don't understand why I'm seeing this. It really scares me."

"Meet me tonight at ten-thirty in the driveway, okay?"

"Mmm-hmm."

"Will you be all right until then?" Ian asked.

"I think so."

I dried my tears and went downstairs. Dad had the TV on, watching a game on ESPN. He was that way. He could watch any sport and enjoy it. He'd signed me up for soccer, t-ball, and basketball when I was little, but I failed at all of them. He was as thrilled as Mom to find out I made the cheerleading squad. That meant he'd have an excuse to go to all the high school football and basketball games.

I passed through without him noticing me and went into Mom's room. I found her sitting up in bed, reading a romance novel.

"Good book?" I muttered.

"Ah, you know, there's a formula to these, so the predictability is enough for me."

"Predictability. Hmm."

"I'm sorry about yesterday. I shouldn't have yelled at you. I'm not ready to go back to Dr. Koman. He has such a disappointed face." She frowned and shook her head. "I'm the personification of his failure."

"I don't think he's trying to cure you. He just wants to help you manage the disorder."

"I hate being managed!" She placed the book on the nightstand and let out a deep sigh. I moved closer to her and she wrapped her arms around me. We sat like that for a while, my head resting on her chest listening to her heart beat.

Dad came into the bedroom as I was leaving. I stood outside the door and listened.

"Are you sleeping here tonight?" Mom asked.

"I have a lot more work to do. Just came down to get some clean shorts," he answered as he closed the drawer.

"I've barely seen you since you got back from the trip."

"I've been here."

"Have you though?" she asked.

"As much as you have."

"I see." She paused. "Work hard then. I'll be here, in bed."

I jumped over to the refrigerator at the sound of Dad walking toward the bedroom door. He didn't even look my way as he walked by. The clock on the microwave read nine-thirty. One more hour until I'd see Ian. I smiled at the thought of it and felt that flip in my stomach, the one that seemed to be happening more and more when he crossed my mind. I knew Hannah would freak if she found out that, not only was I hanging out with Ian, but I really liked him too. I hated the thought of that conversation. In a lot of ways, it would be easier to ignore these feelings and stop hanging out with him. But Ian was the only good thing in my life. He was the raft keeping me afloat in the storm. And I needed his help with these flashbacks. I needed to know what they all meant.

I walked into the living room and fired up my laptop. I signed into Twitter. Zandria was talking to my dad.

@nickray68 you have to talk it out. You'll go crazy if you keep it in.

Was nothing sacred? Were they really doing all of this so publicly? I closed the screen and walked upstairs. Dad's office door was closed, so I knocked.

"Come in," he called.

"What are you working on?"

"The website for that rental property company."

"Is that a big contract?"

"Pretty big." Dad turned his chair to face me. "What about you? What are you doing?"

"I was just goofing online. Thinking of going to bed soon."

"Yeah, I might hit the hay myself here shortly." He glanced over at the stack of pillows and blankets on the couch.

"Why don't you sleep with Mom tonight?" I pushed the bag off the couch and sat down. "It's got to be more comfortable than this."

"This is working okay for me. I kind of like my own space."

"You and Mom have a king-sized bed. There's plenty of space."

"She sleeps fitfully when she's like this." He looked over my head as he spoke.

"And she's been through this at least five times in my life. You've never refused to sleep with her before."

"I can't explain it."

"No, you won't explain it." I got up and walked to the door. I'd hoped he would stop me, but he didn't.

I went to the bathroom and brushed my teeth. I pulled the clip out of my hair and brushed it out. I didn't think Ian had ever seen me with my hair down. It had grown a lot over the summer. I probably needed a cut but neither of my parents had the time or energy to take me. Would it be weird to ask Ian to take me to the salon? That's probably more of a boyfriend request. We were just friends, so it would be weird.

When I came out of the bathroom, Dad was coming up the steps. "Mom asleep?" I asked.

"Yeah and I'm headed there myself." He stopped in the doorway of the office and turned toward me. "Goodnight, Lola. I do love you."

I didn't answer.

It was ten-thirty. I looked out the window. Ian was perched on the tailgate of his truck. I'd have to wait a few minutes before meeting him. I wanted to make sure Dad was asleep before I left.

I was fifteen minutes late when I crossed the street to Ian's driveway. He was laying on the pavement his eyes toward the stars.

"Sometimes I think I just want to run away to a cabin in the woods and spend the rest of my life as a hermit," he said as I approached.

I lay down beside him. "Can I go too? We could be hermits together."

He laughed. "That kind of defeats the purpose, you know?"

"You don't really want to be alone forever, do you?" I sat up and looked down at him.

"Humanity sucks. I'm sick of it." He sat up too and crossed his legs.

"Anything you want to talk about?"

"Not really. Sammy got beat up by a kindergartner in summer camp today. My dad's company is making cuts, your dad's having an affair, and we mustn't forget the unrest in the Middle East and genocides in Africa."

"Wow, I was kind of hoping you'd make me feel better, not worse."

"I'm sorry."

"Don't be. It's not a bad thing. I was just thinking about how cool, calm, and collected you always are. It's nice to see this imperfect side of you."

"Look up imperfect in the dictionary and my picture will be there," he laughed.

"Are you kidding me? It's entirely possible that you might be the best person I've ever met."

"All right, it's official! Let's run away and be communal hermits."

"Okay, but can it wait about eight years? I really want to do that college thing first."

"Fine! College first, then the cabin in the woods." He held out a hand to me.

I shook it. "Deal."

"So tell me about the vision you had," he said, still holding my hand. My face grew hot. I looked down at our hands. He let go and I wondered if he had felt me blush.

"We were waiting in line with the other women and children," I said, trying to forget that jittery feeling in my gut and remember the vision. "The soldiers made us all undress."

"Yeah, they did that for sure." Ian nodded.

"My mother looked so different in that life. She was shorter, much rounder, the complete opposite of how she looks now."

"What did they do to her?" Ian asked.

I shook my head and took a deep breath. I didn't want to start crying again. "I can't say. It was awful. I'm sorry."

"Bastards!" Ian mumbled. "This is exactly what I'm talking about. Screw everyone."

"It happened in the past though. It's over." I stared at him. "What about all the good stuff about humanity? Maybe people aren't really evil, just scared."

"Screw that, Lola! There's nothing worse than the naïve belief that there's no such thing as pure evil. Hitler's evil was so powerful that he infected a mass population of people with it." Ian's voice was infused with anger, hate. He'd never sounded like this before, not even when he talked about the kids at school.

"Why are you so upset?"

He shook his head, picked at the threads of a hole in his jeans. "I've been thinking about your visions, that past life. What if it's not by accident that we moved here the day you first saw it. I mean, I already know I'm supposed to help you, but what if it's because I was there too?"

"I haven't seen you there."

"Are you sure?" He looked up at me. "Cause I really feel connected to you. Like maybe I knew you before now."

"I don't know, Ian. I seem to recognize people even when they look completely different. I haven't recognized you."

"Maybe your subconscious won't let you recognize me."

"What do you mean?"

"Maybe I'm one of the bad guys."

"Absolutely not. You are too good to ever have been bad." I put my arm around his shoulder and gave a quick squeeze. "You're here to be my friend and help me. That's it. There's nothing else to analyze."

"I'm sorry for calling you naïve." Ian reached over and took my hand.

"It's okay."

"I hope we can figure out what you're supposed to get from seeing this past life. It has to be leading you to something."

"Maybe it's leading me to an answer about my family. I mean, I've just never felt so insecure before. And I know that's surprising, considering my mom has been on this bipolar rollercoaster my entire life, but Dad has always stepped in and kept us together. He's totally checked out this time." I leaned back and gazed towards the heavens. "I don't know what I'll do when he leaves."

"When?"

"Yeah, I think we've moved beyond if."

"You'll be just fine, sweetie," Ian said, his gaze following mine. "Look at that sky. It's amazing. We're so tiny in the whole scheme of things."

"Yep, I'm just a minor character in my parent's drama. They barely even see me, yet my life depends on them."

"Don't even talk like that." Ian turned his head and looked at me. "I was talking about The Universe and as small as we may be or feel, every tiny piece is significant."

"Should I tell Dad I know about Zandria?" I asked.

"What do you know though?"

"That they're having an affair and she wants him to tell us about it before he explodes."

"Are you sure that's true?"

I shrugged. "I'll know if I ask."

"Are you prepared to tell him how you know?"

"He probably already knows." I sat up and looked back at Ian. "Besides, I didn't do anything wrong."

"Why so defensive?"

I looked across the street at the dim light coming from my bedroom window. The road was lit by a path of streetlights and the sound of crickets filled the silence. "What time is it?" I asked

Ian after a moment.

"Eleven thirty. Why? You thinking of making a run for it?"

"I wasn't being defensive."

"Okay then. But I can't answer your question about talking to your dad. Only you can do that."

"Do you think they're going to shoot me?"

Ian laughed. "Who? Your dad and Zandria?"

"No! I'm talking about the vision." I stood up and walked to the truck, sat down on the edge.

"There's no telling. They did all kinds of stuff to people."

"I don't want to go back. Don't think I can handle it."

"You're never given more than you can handle."

"Please, don't try to make me feel better with a goofy quote from a meme."

"It's true in this case. If you can't handle a memory from this life or another, it gets blocked. Which is kind of what I was referring to earlier. Maybe you've blocked the memory of me?"

"How do you know all of this?"

"When your mom's a woo-woo therapist, you end up with all kinds of interesting reading material at your disposal. Memory blocks are a defense mechanism. And when people do remember stuff, it's because they're ready to face it. We're pretty intelligent, us humans."

"Well, forgive me, but I don't think I'm ready to face getting shot in the head."

"It's just a dream and you'll wake up. Kind of like this life."

"Dream or not, if feels freakin' real when you're there." Across the street the porch light at my house came on. A panicked feeling rushed over me. "Oh crap!"

Ian ducked into his garage and I ran across the street. The front door opened and Dad came out in a t-shirt and his pajama pants. By the time he saw me, I was sitting in the driveway.

"Lola, what are you doing?" he asked.

"Couldn't sleep, so I came out here to stargaze."

"I went to your room to check on you and you weren't there. You scared the piss out of me."

"Sorry about that. Here I am, though."

"Come inside. It's not safe out here."

"It's not very safe in there either."

"What's that supposed to mean?" Dad sat down beside me.

"Something's changed and I'm not sure what's going to happen to our family. What's going on in your head?" I looked at him.

"We'll talk about it in the morning."

"Who?"

"All of us, okay? You, me, and your mom."

"Are you leaving us?"

"We'll talk in the morning." Dad pulled at the string on his pants.

"Are you moving to Austin?"

"Austin? Why on earth would I move to Austin?"

"I know about her, Dad."

Dad sighed. "Who? Who do you think you know about?"

"Zandria! Your Twitter girlfriend."

"You've got it all wrong. We're friends only."

"Seems to me you're talking to her more than Mom these days." I fought back angry tears.

"She got divorced last year. She's been giving me advice."

"Telling you how to leave us?" I looked down at my trembling hands.

"No, Lola. She's been telling me how to fix us."

"Well, she gives lousy advice because you don't seem to be doing much of anything." I got up and walked to the front door.

Once inside, I didn't bother to walk quietly up the stairs. I doubted Mom would even wake up if the house was on fire. I turned out the light and climbed into bed. A minute later, I heard

Dad on the stairs. He stopped for a moment outside my bedroom door, but didn't come in.

Chapter 15

The next morning, I found Mom and Dad sitting at the kitchen table together drinking coffee. They sat there in silence as I walked in. Mom's eyes were red. My presence in the room startled them. Mom jumped up and moved toward the counter, hiding her face with her hair.

"Lola, can I get you something for breakfast?" Her voice was shaky.

I looked back and forth between their grief-stricken faces. I reached out and grasped the nearest chair as a sick feeling washed over me. "What's going on? What did I miss?"

"Tell her, Nick."

Dad shook his head and stared at his coffee mug. He was too chicken to even look at me.

"Your father wants to move out. Separate." Mom carefully poured another cup of coffee.

I wanted to slap him. How could he do this to us? "So you are leaving us? Why didn't you just tell me so last night?"

"I needed to tell your mother first." Dad leaned back, ran his hands through his thinning hair.

"So when are you going?" I could feel the blood pumping through my veins.

"Today," Mom answered quickly.

I looked at Dad. "Are you kidding me?"

"Leaving today was not my decision. It was hers." Dad pointed to Mom. "I was going to wait till the weekend."

"If you're leaving, I want you out today. Hell, I want you out NOW!" Mom gripped the mug with both hands like she was resisting the urge to throw it. As much as I didn't want Dad to leave, she had a point. How could we spend the next few days with him here, knowing he had already left? Wouldn't it just be salt in the wound? But how could she kick him out now, before I'd even been included in the discussion?

"You guys are so selfish," I shouted.

"He's the selfish one!" Mom yelled even louder than me. "What have you been doing Nick, having an affair? Is that why you stopped sleeping in our bed? You leaving me for some other woman?"

"Are you kidding me? Our entire life together has been this insanity. I'm so sick of the highs and the lows. Have we ever had an in-between? I just can't do it anymore. It's damn exhausting." A look of surrender washed over him. "But, yeah sure, let's just ignore the obvious and accuse good ole Nick of having an affair. You and Lola both. The craziness that has been this marriage can't possibly be the reason I want to leave. If thinking I'm having an affair makes you feel better, go ahead and think it." Dad got up and left the room. As angry as I was, I also felt sorry for him. He was right. He'd taken on a lot when he married Mom.

"Where the hell are you going?" Mom screamed after him.

"To pack!"

Mom stormed out of the kitchen and into her bedroom. She slammed the door so hard a picture fell off the wall. At least it was canvas, so it didn't shatter. I collapsed into the chair I had been gripping and let my forehead fall to the table. The bomb had just gone off. Now what?

I skipped breakfast and went up to my room to call Ian. Dad stood at his desk, packing his laptop into a messenger bag. His black gym bag sat on the couch, seemingly full. Our eyes met for a moment as I stood motionless in the hall. I could see that he was crying. In my room, I grabbed the phone and sat on the floor, my back against the closed door.

"Hello."

"Hi, Mr. White. Is Ian there?"

"Hi, Lola! How are you this morning?"

"I'm good, thank you," I lied.

"It's good to hear that. Now let me just put my son on the line for you."

"Hey," Ian said. "I've been thinking about you all morning. Did you get in trouble last night? I've been worried I got you into a jam."

"Last night?" I'd almost forgotten. "Oh, yeah. No, no trouble."

"Then what's wrong? You sound like someone just died."

"Dad's packing as we speak."

"Packing for another business trip, I hope."

"No, he's leaving. I woke up this morning and he and Mom were in the kitchen talking about it."

"Did he mention Twitter lady?"

"I asked him about her last night. He said they're just friends. Mom accused him of an affair this morning, but he denies it."

"Do you believe him?" Ian asked.

"I think so." I paused. "You've been through this. What happens now?"

"I don't know. It's different for everyone. My parents talked about it for a long time and had everything worked out before they told Sammy and me. No one was angry. Dad just moved to an apartment one day. He and Mom were always nice to each other. Once he was settled, we started switching off the weeks."

"My mom's pissed."

"That does not surprise me."

"I'm not sure what she's going to do."

"Forget about her for a minute. How do you feel?"

"Shocked. Mad. Sad. But not terrified like I thought I'd be."

"Do you want me to come over?" Ian asked.

"That's okay. I'll be fine."

"Promise to call me if you aren't fine?"

"I promise."

"Lola, just know that I am always here for you."

"I know," I answered.

I hung up the phone and looked around the room. With all the stress I was feeling, I needed to stay busy. If I happened to lie down, I might slip back into a vision and things were bad enough as they were. I couldn't handle a visit to the death camp. The bookshelf caught my attention so I decided to reorganize it. After all the books were alphabetized by title instead of author, I moved on to my drawers. I cleaned out all the clothes I hadn't worn in the last year and put them in a bag to donate. Finally, I took out the vacuum and practiced my deep breathing as I made new lines. The room was spotless, so I moved on to the bathroom. When I opened my bedroom door, Dad was standing with his fist up, ready to knock.

"I'm going to go now."

"Where to?"

"Gonna see if the Holiday Inn can take me a few days early, I guess."

I threw myself into his arms and sobbed. He held me for a long time. When we finally let go, he reached over and wiped the tears off my cheek. His eyes were red and puffy too. "You'll be okay. We'll get this all figured out. Please just know how much I love you and that this is definitely not about you." His hand was under my chin, forcing me to look into his eyes.

"I love you too." I leaned into him again.

"Come on. Walk me out."

He'd pulled his car out of the garage already. We stepped toward it and I saw the backseat holding his most necessary possessions: a stack of files, the gym bag turned overnight bag, his laptop computer, and my school picture in a frame.

"I don't want you to go," I cried as he climbed into the car.

"If I stay, I'll have a nervous breakdown." He reached up from the driver's seat and gripped my hand.

"What about me?"

"You're stronger than you think and I'm going to be around for you. I promise."

He pulled slowly out of the driveway. I sat down on the concrete and hugged my knees. This was it. Just like I'd imagined, Dad was gone. I ignored the urge to run, screaming after his car, and just lowered my head and wept.

"Lola? You okay?" I looked up to see Ian sprinting across the street. "Sammy told me you were out here."

I wiped the tears from my face. "I didn't even see him."

"He'd just gone out to check the mail and saw you."

"Your Dad gone?"

"Yeah, he just left." I leaned back and took a deep breath.

Ian sat down beside me. "Where's he going?"

"Hotel."

"How's your mom?"

"I have no idea." I looked toward the house. "I'm scared to find out."

"But I thought she'd barely spoken to him in weeks."

"That doesn't mean she wants him to leave. She gets in these ruts and she neglects him. But she still loves him and needs him.

He was different this time around, but I don't think she thought he'd really leave." I wrapped my arms around my knees again and rocked. "What if she doesn't snap out of it this time?"

"Maybe you should go check on her."

"I guess." I stumbled getting to my feet. Ian reached for my arm and balanced me.

"See you later," he said, standing in front of me.

I leaned into him, pressed my cheek to his chest. He wrapped his arms around me. "Thank you," I whispered.

He brushed his hand across my hair. "I'd do anything for you." The words spilled out before he could stop them.

"I'd better go." I stared into his eyes and smiled before walking away. I'd never known anyone like him before. In that moment, he'd managed to ease the pain a bit. I opened the front door slowly and took a deep breath.

"What was that?" Mom had been watching from the window. "You begging your father to take you with him? Crying with your boyfriend because he wouldn't?"

"No. That wasn't it at all."

"Your bastard father deceiving me doesn't surprise me one bit. But you? How could you?" She stopped in front of me, with wild eyes, her whole body shaking. "You're just an ungrateful little brat."

"What are you talking about, Mom? I'm right here. WITH YOU!" I pushed past her toward the stairs. She followed me.

"Please, don't leave me, Lola!" She started to cry.

I turned around and walked back down the stairs. Her eyes were red, her face streaked with tears. I reached out and touched a strand of her blonde hair. It was oily and dull. "I'm not going anywhere. I love you and we're going to be fine."

She collapsed onto the step and leaned against the wall. "I didn't think he'd really do it. I mean, I felt it, but didn't want to believe it. We've always struggled and he's always stood strong."

She gazed around the room with a look of confusion. "I was always honest with him about my issues. I warned him from the very beginning that I was going to be hard to live with. He said he didn't care. He promised me forever."

"Maybe he'll change his mind," I mumbled, willing to say anything to make her better.

"He won't. He never makes decisions lightly. He's a man of his word. Always." Her voice trailed off. "Maybe I should call Dr. Koman."

"Come on, Mom. Let me make you something to eat." I reached my hand to her and led her off of the stairs and into the kitchen. Her last statement lingered in my mind, a small thread of hope.

Mom sat at the table quietly sobbing while I fixed two grilled cheese sandwiches and simmered a can of tomato soup on the stove. I'd have to save my tears for later. She needed me to be the strong one now.

Chapter 16

"Lola." Mom's footsteps moved closer to my bed. I opened my eyes to see her opening the curtains at the window. "I'm making breakfast, honey. How many pancakes do you want?"

"Are you all right?" I looked at her. She was bright-eyed and smiling. I was confused.

"I'm great! I got to thinking last night that Dad leaving is for the best. This is my second chance. . . our second chance." She reached her hand out to me. I glared suspiciously before finally taking it. "Now, how many pancakes?"

"Three?" I tossed the covers back and climbed out of bed.

"Three it is! They'll be ready in five." She glided out of the room.

Was it possible that she could be this okay with everything? You do hear about people having aha moments that change them forever. Could Dad leaving be her cure? Unlikely. I looked out the window, catching a glimpse of Ian's truck. It was his last two days at his Dad's. I'd come to dread the days when he moved over to Joan's house.

I stepped into the bathroom, brushed my teeth and twisted my hair into a bun. I could smell the aroma of turkey bacon and eggs from downstairs. I was even pretty sure I heard Mom humming a tune. This was not normal.

"There you go." She pointed to the table as I entered the kitchen. "What would you like to drink?"

"Water's fine." I moved toward the cabinet to get a glass.

"Let me do that." She nudged me back to the table. "And you need some vitamin C. I want you to have orange juice."

"Come on, what's up with you?" Mom wasn't behaving rationally. If there was one day when she should be in bed, paralyzed by fear and anxiety, it was this day—the day after her husband walked out.

"I'm taking care of my daughter. Is that okay with you?" She placed the juice in front of me and kissed my head. A moment later, she joined me at the table with her cup of coffee.

"Where's yours?" I pointed to the empty space where her plate of pancakes and bacon should have been.

"Not hungry. This is good for now." She lifted her coffee mug in the air. "So, tell me about Ian. You two an item now?"

"We're just friends." I felt my face grow hot.

Mom laughed. "That's not exactly the look one gets when they're talking about a friend."

"It's complicated, though."

"What's complicated? If you like him, you like him."

"He's such a good friend. I don't want to mess anything up." I stabbed at the pancakes with my fork. "Besides, Hannah thinks he's weird. If she finds out, she'll never let me live it down."

"Hannah's a spoiled brat," Mom replied.

"She's my best friend."

"That doesn't make her any less of a brat." Mom walked over to the coffee pot and refilled her cup. "I think you should tell him you like him.

Why were we even having this conversation? Dad was gone.

"I don't know if I like him."

"Of course, you do. It's written all over your face."

"Can we change the subject, please?" I put my fork down and looked in Mom's eyes. "Are you really all right?"

She smiled and took a sip of her coffee. "I'm fine, I promise."

I realized I needed to grant my own request and change the subject. "What's on the agenda today?"

"I have an appointment with Dr. Koman after lunch," Mom answered.

"That's great! What time do I need to be ready?"

"I'd really like to do this one on my own. I've got to be more independent now." She turned around and leaned against the counter.

"Are you sure?"

"Definitely."

"We should go out to dinner tonight. Do something to mark this occasion. Celebrate our independence!" I smiled at her, hoping she was buying the act. The last thing I wanted to do was celebrate Dad being gone.

"I was thinking of going to the studio this afternoon. I'm feeling inspired. Don't want to lose this idea. I'll probably be back in time for dinner, but I don't want to make any promises."

I carried my plate to the sink. "That's okay. I'm glad you want to work. In fact, that's fabulous. You should definitely do that." I reached over and squeezed her hand.

"We really are going to be okay, Lola," she called as I left the room.

Upstairs, I climbed in the shower and cried. How could she think we'd be okay?

After Mom left for her appointment, I went over to Ian's house. "Ah, I see you received my signals," he said as he let me in.

"Signals?"

"I've been thinking about you all morning. Was going to call you."

"So why didn't you?"

"Uh, I don't, uh, know," he stuttered and his face turned bright red.

"What's going on, weirdo?" I punched him playfully.

He grabbed his arm and let out an exaggerated groan. "Nothing, nothing. So, how's your mom? Did you talk to your dad today?"

"Don't change the subject. What's really on your mind?" We walked into the living room and I plopped into the red recliner. Sammy zoomed through, pretending to be an airplane.

"I'm scared shitless to say," Ian replied.

"Oooooh, I'm going to tell Dad you said a bad word," Sammy shouted from across the room.

Ian threw a pillow at him. "Get out of here, li'l man!"

My heart dropped to my stomach as I stared at Ian. "What's to be scared of? It's me you're talking to."

"Exactly. It's you, my best friend, and I don't want to screw anything up."

A lump formed in my throat. "You won't." That was all that came out even though I wanted to say more, like that I felt like he was my best friend too.

Ian shook his head. "Nah, know what? Just forget I said anything at all. It's not a good time for this, with your parents and stuff."

"You have got to be kidding me? After all that lead-up, I can't forget you said anything. And as far as my parents go, I could really use a distraction from that problem."

"All right, fine. Here goes nothing." He squeezed his eyes closed. "Would you like to go to dinner with me tonight?"

My chest felt tight, like my heart had expanded or something. Was Ian really asking me out? Did he feel about me the way I did about him? His green eyes seemed lit up in a new way. A bead of sweat trailed his hairline. "Sure, I'll go to dinner with you."

"Yeah?"

"Of course," I laughed.

"You do realize I mean dinner as in a dinner DATE, right?"

My stomach flipped. "I was hoping that's what you meant." My face grew hot. I couldn't believe I'd just said that.

Relief spread across his face. "Awesome."

Ian and I spent the next couple of hours playing video games and watching TV. We decided to leave for dinner at seven o'clock. I went home to get ready.

Mom wasn't back yet. I checked the answering machine, hoping for a message about her appointment, but the light wasn't blinking. I tried to call her studio. No answer. I called her cell and, of course, it wasn't turned on. Her "emergency only" cell phone may as well have been a Barbie phone.

I hoped she'd get home soon. I wanted to share this occasion with her. It was my first date and I hadn't even told her about it yet. Technically, I wasn't even sure if I was allowed to date, but it was Ian and that made it different.

I went upstairs to get ready. I brushed my hair out and plugged in the flat iron. While I waited for it to heat up, I debated putting on makeup. Was that trying too hard? Ian had never seen me in makeup. Would I be setting a precedent for all our future encounters or would I just be honoring this special occasion by going an extra mile? I smeared the creamy foundation on my face, deciding the extra effort would mean a lot. After straightening my hair, I went to my room and stared into the closet. What to wear?

I decided on capri-length leggings and a t-shirt dress with a belt around it. It was a little nicer looking then my usual shorts and t-shirt, but still comfy. I looked at my reflection in the full-length mirror then grabbed the phone to try once more to reach

Mom. Ian would be here in ten minutes.

Mom still didn't answer the phone at her studio. I was overwhelmed with worry for a moment, but assured myself this was normal. In fact, this was a good thing. Not only was Mom out of bed, but she was getting lost in her art again. After all, it was standard practice for her to turn off the ringer on the phone when she was in the zone. And she did say she couldn't make any promises for dinner.

I hung up the phone and went down to the kitchen. The doorbell rang as I fumbled through the junk drawer, looking for a pen to write a note. I shoved the drawer closed and ran to the door.

Ian's face changed when he saw me. "Wow," he said. He was wearing black jeans and his black Converse sneakers. He had on a striped button-down shirt, with a red t-shirt peeking out from underneath, and he wore the fedora he had on the first time we met.

"I haven't seen that in a while." I pointed to the hat.

"It's for special occasions only."

"Special occasions? The last time I saw you wear it, you were moving boxes and sweating."

"Moving day was a special occasion." He smiled. "You look incredible, by the way. What's different?"

I shielded my face with my hands. "I suppose it could be the makeup I put on."

Ian clutched his chest and staggered. "You put on makeup for me."

"Shut up!" I shoved him gently.

"I'm sorry. You really do look great. You always do though." He looked down at his feet. "Anyway, uh, you ready?"

"Yeah, I was gonna write my mom a note, but I suppose I can just call and leave her a message in a bit. Let me just go get my stuff." Ian stepped inside as I hopped up the steps to my room. I reached in the jewelry box on my nightstand, grabbed a twenty and put it in the little clutch bag Hannah had given me last Christmas. This was only the third time I'd had an excuse to use the bag.

"Hope you don't mind walking to my driveway," Ian said. "It seemed pointless to move the truck across the street."

I stopped in my tracks. "That's it. I don't think I can go out with you."

"What?" Panic filled Ian's voice.

"I'm just kidding," I laughed. "You should see your face. Wow."

"I was planning to open the car door for you, but I think you just changed my mind. I'm not sure you've earned my chivalry." Ian approached the truck and opened the passenger door. "Just kidding," he said as he gestured toward the seat.

"Thank you." I smiled and climbed in the truck.

"So where is your mom anyway?" Ian asked as he started the engine.

"Believe it or not, she went to the doctor and to her art studio today."

"That's great!"

"I hope it is. She was a totally new woman this morning. She even made me pancakes."

"That's very good."

"Almost too good to be true."

"Have you heard from your dad?"

"He sent me an email saying he was at the hotel."

"An email?" Ian scrunched up his face. "Isn't that a little . . ."

"Impersonal? Yeah, but I think he was just scared to call. Scared to upset Mom. Scared to face the reality." I looked out the window as Ian turned into the parking lot of Tony's.

"How's this?" He pointed to the restaurant.

"My favorite."

"What a coincidence," he smiled.

I opened the door and let myself out before Ian made it around to do it for me. When I got out of the car, he reached for my hand. I couldn't believe I felt this way about Ian. I could have burst right there. I wondered if he felt it, too. The excitement, the nervousness. His hand felt nice, warm. It's strange how much a relationship can shift in a moment. We walked toward the door, hand-in-hand. I reminded myself to breathe.

When we entered Tony's, I sat down next to another family waiting and Ian went to give them our name. "Twenty minutes," he announced when he joined me on the booth.

"That's not too bad for a Friday night," I said.

"White, party of two," the hostess called after about five minutes of awkward silence.

"Quick twenty minutes." Ian sounded as nervous as I was.

Just as we headed to our table, someone I knew entered the front door—Hannah's mom and stepdad. I pulled my hair around to hide my face as we followed the hostess. I could almost hear my heart beating. As much as I liked being here with Ian, I didn't want her to recognize me. I didn't want Hannah to know about this date. I'd tell her when I was ready, when I was sure it was worth her reaction.

Ian and I sat at a table in the corner near the hallway to the restrooms. "This is nice," he said as we looked at the menus.

"Haven't you been here before?"

"Not in a long time." He put his menu down. "I think I'm going with the chicken parm. What about you?"

"Gorgonzola mushroom ravioli for me."

"You daredevil, you," he smiled. "Which reminds me, have you had any more dreams?"

"No, not in a while. Now that Dad's gone, maybe they're done. I've seen all I've needed to see to accept him leaving."

"Maybe."

Across the restaurant, I saw Hannah's mom walking this way. I felt a burst of adrenaline. I looked around the room, trying to figure out if there was anywhere to go or any place to hide.

"Lola, are you okay?" Ian asked.

"I'm fine."

"You don't look fine. You either look like you just saw a ghost or are about to puke. Or both."

Just then, Mrs. Stalls approached our table. "Lola Ray! How has your summer been going?"

"Hi, Mrs. Stalls. I'm good. Summer's good. How are you?"

"Well, you know, I'm missing my baby. As I'm sure you are, too."

"When is she coming home?" I asked nervously.

"You don't know? I assumed you two would have been talking up a storm all summer." She glanced at Ian. "Hannah will be back in three weeks."

"Okay, I do think I knew that. It's been a crazy, busy summer. We haven't talked as much as I'd hoped and since my mom still won't let me have a cell, texting is out."

Hannah's mom's eyes fixed on Ian. "Who's your friend? Hannah didn't tell me you have a boyfriend."

"Well, no, um, this is actually my neighbor, Ian."

"Hi there, Ian. Now are you friends with my daughter, Hannah?"

"I've actually not had the chance to get to know your daughter yet, though I've heard wonderful things from Lola here," Ian replied.

"She and Lola go way back, since grade school." Mrs. Stalls looked from Ian to me and smiled. "Okay, I'll let you two get back to your dinner. It was great seeing you, Lola. I'll be sure to tell Hannah you said hi."

"Your neighbor?" Ian said after she walked away.

"What did you want me to say? One date doesn't make you

my boyfriend."

"How about friend? You could have introduced me as your friend." Ian's face flushed with disappointment.

"I'm sorry."

"You're embarrassed of me, aren't you? You don't want Hannah to know we actually are friends."

"That's not true. I'm not embarrassed of you," I lied.

Ian pushed back from the table and shook his head. "I'm not stupid, Lola. And you're no different than the rest of the jerks you hang out with."

Chapter 17

The rest of our dinner date was overshadowed by uncomfortable silence. It was the first time since I'd met Ian that I'd felt so awkward in his presence. It had started out as an exciting, hopeful awkwardness, but had morphed into a mortifying awkward. I'd screwed up, big time. Why did I care so much what Hannah thought? In some twisted way, I always felt that Hannah had the power to make or break me. She was the popular one, the one people listened to and cared about. For years, I'd been riding on her coat tails, coasting along and fitting in. Fitting in was easy and comfortable. And with everything going on at home, a completely normal life so unlikely, I needed at least one part of it to be easy. But I did like Ian, a lot.

When the check came, I pulled the twenty out of my purse and handed it to Ian.

"I've got this." He pushed the money back toward me.

"The least I can do is pay for my half."

"This is still a date, even if it's not a good one." He held the money out to the waitress as she passed.

"Please don't be mad at me, Ian." I stared in his eyes.

"I'm not mad. This is nothing new." His voice broke and he stood up quickly. "I need to go to the bathroom."

I watched him walk down the hallway to the restrooms. His head moved around a little. I'm pretty sure he was talking to himself. Probably saying the same thing I was. *What is wrong with you? How could you screw things up this badly?* I should have never agreed to this date. I wanted him in my life even if we were just friends. I shouldn't have risked that.

Ian returned from the bathroom and dropped some cash on the table for tip. "You ready?" he asked.

I took one last sip of my water and nodded.

On the drive home, Ian turned the music way up. I could barely hear myself think and definitely didn't bother to speak. He turned into my driveway and turned off the engine. "Well, here we are."

"Yep."

"I would walk you to the door, but, you know, someone might see you with me and we know how that is."

"I'm sorry." The words squeaked out right before the tears started to fall. I jumped out of the car quickly, before Ian noticed I was crying, and ran to the front door. To my surprise, he stayed parked in the driveway as I fidgeted with the keys and unlocked the door. I looked back toward the truck one more time as I pushed open the door.

The house was very quiet as I walked in. All I wanted to do was run to my room and cry myself to sleep. I looked around the room, and under the dim light of the lamp, I saw her lying on the couch. An empty wine bottle sat on the coffee table and next to it laid a bottle of pills, opened, with the contents strewn across the surface. I ran toward her. "Mom, Mom! Wake up!"

She didn't move. I put my arms around her and lifted her. She still didn't wake. I tried to find her pulse, but couldn't. I picked up the bottle. It was a new prescription of sleeping pills.

Half of them were gone. I ran to the kitchen and grabbed the phone. 9-1-1.

"My mom won't wake up. She took pills. Please come now." I dropped the phone and ran to the front door. Ian's truck was in his driveway now. He walked toward the garage. "Ian! Ian! It's my mom, help!"

"What?" he yelled back.

"Please, I think she's dead!" I screamed. He sprinted toward me.

"What's going on?" he asked as he reached the front stoop. I stood back and let him in.

"I think she's tried to kill herself. I just found her like this." I knelt beside the couch and put my arms around her. My entire body was shaking. "Mom, Mom, please wake up."

"Is she breathing?" Ian moved closer.

"I think so, but she won't wake up and I can't find her pulse." I laid my head on her chest. "I can't hear her heart beating."

Right then, we heard the sirens outside. "You called 911?" Ian asked.

I ran out the front door to meet the paramedics. They followed me back into the house. "I think she tried to commit suicide," I cried.

The men ran to her side and began working on her. I stood horrified across the room, watching and sobbing. Ian wrapped his arms around me. "She's still alive. She's going to be okay."

"I forgot to call her. It's my fault. I didn't wait for her to get home. I didn't call her. I didn't even leave a note. She was so happy this morning and I ruined it. It's all my fault."

"This your mom?" a paramedic yelled as they pushed the gurney out the front door. "You coming with us?"

"Yes, I'm coming." I pulled away from Ian and ran after them.

"Where's your Dad?" Ian called.

"At the Holiday Inn on the parkway."

"I'll call him for you."

"Thank you," I replied before climbing in the back of the ambulance with my mom.

When we got to the hospital, I was sent to a waiting room while they worked on Mom. Dad arrived about thirty minutes after we did.

"How is she?" he asked as he burst into the room and took me in his arms.

"Alive," I replied before completely losing it.

"I'm so sorry you had to find her like that. I wish it would have been me instead of you." He walked me to the chairs that lined the wall and we sat.

"She was good this morning. She was out of bed, making breakfast and happy even. I wanted to believe she was fine. She went to the studio and stayed gone all day. Ian and I made plans to go to dinner and I couldn't reach her to tell her I was going out." I shook my head. "I should have waited for her."

"It's not your fault."

The doctor came into the waiting room. "Mr. Ray?" He looked at Dad.

"Yes."

"We pumped her stomach. She is conscious and resting now."

"Can we see her? Is she talking?" I asked.

"She did answer some questions for us," the doctor replied.

"Did she do it on purpose?" Dad asked.

The doctor shrugged. "She tells us it was accidental. Do you have any reason not to believe that?"

"Can we see her?" I asked before Dad could answer the doctor's question.

"Follow me." The doctor led us down the hall to her room.

Dad stopped outside the door to the room. "I'll wait out

here."

I took a deep breath and stepped into the hospital room. "Hi, Mom. How ya feeling?" I stepped toward her bed and gently ran my hand across her forehead.

She opened her eyes and looked at me. "I'm so sorry. I swear it was an accident." A tear slipped out of her eye. "I was so worried about you that I worked myself into a panic attack. I tried to calm myself down. That's all I wanted to do was relax."

I started to cry again. "I'm so sorry, Mom. I should have told you where I went."

"Shhh, baby. It's not your fault."

"I tried to call you at the studio and I didn't take the time to write a note. It is my fault. I just forgot to check in with you."

Tears flowed from Mom's eyes now, too. She pulled my hand to her lips and kissed it.

"I promise to never mess up like this again. Please don't leave me." I crawled into the bed beside her.

She stroked my hair. "Does your father know we're here?"

I nodded. "He's in the hall."

"Oh, great. This must really look bad." She patted my arm and pressed the button to raise the bed. "Go get your Dad. I need to explain."

I went to the door and gestured Dad inside. "Christine." He nodded and approached the bed. "You okay?" I watched him with her. There was love in his eyes, or perhaps it was just concern.

"I'm sorry you got dragged into this, Nick. I was worried about Lola and had some wine to relax." She paused for a moment, wiped the tears from her eyes. "The wine didn't work, so I took a couple of sleeping pills to fend off the panic attack."

"A couple?" He placed his hand on hers and shook his head. He still loved her.

She reached up and stroked his face. "I'm really okay. I don't want you second-guessing your decision."

A tear slipped down his cheek, he wiped it with his shoulder. "I can come back home, Christine." My heart fluttered.

"Why? So we can do this whole thing again a few months from now? It took you years to get the balls to leave. I don't need you coming back now." Mom turned her face toward the window and blinked back her tears. "I'm not suicidal. I'll be fine."

"When are they letting you out of this place?"

"Assuming the psyche eval goes okay—and it will—I'll be out tomorrow or the next day."

"Well, I'll stay at the house with Lola until you're out," Dad replied. The small glimmer of hope was crushed. They were going to carry on, separately.

It was after midnight when Dad and I left the hospital. Rain pounded the windshield as we drove. I leaned my head back and closed my eyes. It had arguably been the most emotionally exhausting day of the summer and that was saying a lot.

The sound of crying rang in my head. I hoped it was just the sound of the windshield wipers, but I knew it wasn't.

Mother sobs and screams beside me. "Why? Why? Why would they do this?" The gun is cold against my temple. No one is looking at my mother anymore. Humiliation has turned to excruciating fear. The soldier calls to another soldier. "Take this defiant piece of filth." A young man approaches. The same young soldier who helped me into the train car at the station. His eyes are sweet and pure, yet he wears the uniform of evil. I am on my knees and he lifts me up by my arm. He looks at me in a way no one has before. It's as if he sees my soul. "You will shoot her!" the older man yells. I look back to see him jerk my mother up on both feet. He puts the gun to her throat and is telling her to watch. "Watch your daughter die," he says, laughing. My mother

shrieks and wails. The young man has his gun on me now. His hands are shaking. I look in his eyes and know he is as scared as I am.

"Lola, Lola, we're home!" Dad squeezed my knee to wake me. "Are you okay? It seems like you were having an awfully bad dream."

I opened my eyes to see the car lights shining on the front of the garage door. I wasn't going to die today. Relief washed over me. I opened the car door and climbed out. Dad placed his arm around my shoulder, holding an umbrella over my head, and guided me to the front door.

"Lola!" I heard Ian's voice behind me.

I looked over my shoulder to see him standing in the driveway, his hair wet from the rain. "Don't be too long." Dad handed me the umbrella and went inside.

I walked to Ian.

"Is she okay?"

"Yeah. She swears it was an accident. I think I believe her."

"Are you all right?"

"I can't tell yet," I muttered. "Thank you for helping tonight."

Ian put his arms around me. I pressed my face into his chest, feeling the cool of his damp t-shirt on my cheek. "You're the best friend I've ever had, Lola. I don't want that to change. I'm sorry for being such a wuss tonight. I want you to know I'm here for you no matter what. I'll never ask for more than your friendship again."

"You didn't do anything wrong. It was my fault." Ian put his finger up to my lips.

"It's over now. Let's make a promise here and now not to talk about it anymore." He put his hand out. "Friends?"

"Friends," I agreed and shook his hand.

"Now get to bed. I'll talk to you tomorrow." He pulled me toward him and kissed the top of my head. It felt so good, so honest.

"Thanks again." I stood under the umbrella, watching him sprint up his driveway. I touched the place on my head he'd just kissed as he disappeared into the garage.

I placed the wet umbrella on the welcome mat and stepped into my house. The place I'd found Mom seemed to have a spotlight on it. I walked over and sat down on the couch, elbows on thighs, and rested my forehead in my hands. I was still stunned. As I stared at the floor, I spotted a pill beneath the coffee table. I picked it up and tried to imagine how she felt. What does that kind of panic feel like? Then I remembered the dream and the terror I'd felt the moment before Dad woke me.

Chapter 18

Mom came home from the hospital on Sunday afternoon. We had dinner together as a family and then Dad went back to the hotel. Dr. Koman agreed that the overdose was accidental and assured Dad that sticking to the planned separation was probably better for all of us in the long run. We needed consistency. If Dad came back home only to leave again later on, it would just be more painful. I secretly hoped Mom's accident was a wake-up call that would bring him home for good. I thought, at the very least, Dad would want to shield me from the possibility of a repeat experience. He'd really made up his mind, though. If a near-death occurrence couldn't bring him home, nothing would.

Monday morning, I found Mom in the kitchen eating a bowl of cereal and studying the pamphlets for her new medicine. "You're up early this morning," she said.

"Seems we both are."

"Well, you know, it's time for me to grab the wheel here." She waved the pamphlet in the air. "Side effects may not be so bad with this new one Dr. Koman gave me."

"That's good." I poured some raisin bran into a bowl and joined Mom at the table.

"I'm really sorry that you found me like that. I—" she reached across the table and placed her hand on mine, "I just can't imagine how that must have felt."

"I'm just glad it was an accident." I looked at her. "I really need you. I don't know what I'd do without you."

"I know, baby." She wiped a tear from her eye and took her empty bowl to the sink. "How are things going with your friend?"

"Ian?"

"Yes, Ian. Did you tell him how you felt?"

"We actually attempted a date on Friday night."

She looked up from the sink. "A date? You went on your first date?"

"Well, attempted is the operative word. It sort of turned into a disaster."

"Was it a disaster before or after you found your mother half-dead in the living room?" she laughed.

I shook my head.

"Too soon to joke about it?" she asked.

"Definitely too soon."

"So tell me, what happened?" She walked back to the table.

"We ran into Hannah's mom and I freaked out and introduced him as my neighbor."

"There's nothing wrong with that. What's wrong with that? It's the truth. He is your neighbor."

"He's also the best friend I've ever had. I could have at least said friend." I stared at the soggy flakes in my cereal bowl. "I really hurt his feelings."

"If he's a real friend, he'll forgive you."

"Well, assuming he does forgive me, I'm done trying to be more than friends. I'm just crossing my fingers that I haven't screwed up what we had before."

"It'll be fine," Mom said.

"I don't know. After what I did, I'm having a hard time

imagining playing video games with him now."

"You're over-thinking things. Just let it go. The past is the past. Nothing you can do to change it." She took my bowl from the table to wash it. "Would you like to go to the studio with me today?"

"I'd love to."

I walked into the small studio space and looked around at Mom's work. One painting in the corner of the room caught my eye. It was of a nude woman and an older child, a girl. The woman was on the ground, distraught, holding her daughter in her arms. As I looked closer, I saw the daughter was crying tears of blood. The background was red with yellow stars. There was great fear coming through the full-figured woman's face.

"Mom, when did you do this one?" I asked.

"Last January, I believe."

"Who is it?"

"I don't know. I just get these morbid thoughts sometimes. One day, I had a flash of this woman holding her dying daughter. It was horrifying and beautiful. I painted it."

"I think it's us," I whispered.

She stood next to me examining the painting. "I suppose, if you consider what happened to us Friday night, the mother *could* be symbolic of you and the child me," she paused, "our roles reversed."

"No, I mean it's actually us. I think I've seen this or at least what comes before this."

"What are you talking about?"

"It's our past life together, Mom."

"Past life?" Mom paused. "You mean as in reincarnation?"

I nodded.

She put her hand on my back and looked at me. "I know this summer has been hard for you, but what you're saying sounds . . .

crazy."

"Lots of people believe in reincarnation and past lives."

"Trust me, you don't want to say this kind of thing to just anyone. Once you get a label, it's nearly impossible to shed."

"It's not crazy."

"Okay. So . . . I'll humor you for a minute. Tell me what you know about the painting."

"You, me, and Dad were a family, just like now but we were Jews. We ended up on a train with hundreds of others to a concentration camp. When we got there, we were separated from Dad. We lined up with all the other women and children and had to undress. You looked like that." I pointed to the picture. "This one guard was messing with you and I screamed for him to stop and leave you alone. They put a gun to my head and pulled me out of line. I think they killed me in front of you." I swallowed back the urge to cry.

"My, oh my. You do have a wild imagination," Mom shook her head, but pulled me in for a hug. "You should write all this down. It would make a great story."

"It's not a story, I swear. I've been there. Remember the train in DC? When I passed out? That was the first time I remembered and I keep going back. Ian says I'm seeing it all for a reason. That life relates to this one. If I see what happened to our family then, I can understand why things are happening now."

"Oh, dear. Perhaps it is for the best things didn't go so well with Ian the other night. He sounds like he's just going to lead you to the loony bin."

"I am not crazy and neither is he. I'm the same age now as I was then. The same person who took Dad away from us then is the one that triggered him to leave us now."

Mom stopped and stared at me. "Wait, what did you say? No one triggered your father to leave us. He said he didn't have an affair. What do you know?"

I felt fear rise inside of me. I'd said too much. "I don't know anything. Forget I said that."

"Who triggered him to leave, Lola?" Mom grabbed my shoulders and looked at me.

"No one."

"Don't lie to me."

This was bad. I didn't want to tell her about Zandria, but she would know I was lying. What would the truth do to her? I took a breath and answered, "It was a woman named Zandria. He met her on Twitter. He didn't cheat on you, though. They're just friends."

"How do you know about all of this? Did he tell you? I can't believe the two of you, always going behind my back." She paced back and forth in the studio.

"No one went behind your back. I found out by accident because she emailed him one day when I was cleaning his office. So I started following her on Twitter to watch when she talked to Dad. When I really felt like Dad was thinking of leaving us, I asked him about her and he swore to me they've only been friends."

"She didn't trigger him to leave then."

"But he was talking to her instead of you." I looked down at the floor. "I think he realized other people will be there for him. He doesn't need to count on just you and me anymore. Other people care about him, too. That's the trigger."

"And what about me? Who's going to be there for me?" Mom slid down the wall and rested her head on her knees.

"I'm here for you." I sat down beside her and put my head on her shoulder. While she cried, I thought about the two of us and how much we needed each other now. Maybe Dad would still come back to us, but if not, we needed to pull ourselves together.

Chapter 19

After the trip to the studio, all I wanted to do was talk to Ian about the painting. If he'd been at his dad's, it might have been easier, but this was his mom's week. Even though he claimed he forgave me, I was too afraid to call. I decided to send an email instead.

I told him about the painting, about how much it resembled the mother and daughter we were in the concentration camp. I wrote about Mom's reaction, the way she called me crazy. I didn't tell him she blamed him for most of it. But I did tell him how I let Zandria's name slip and that I hadn't wanted Mom to know about that. Part of me thought it would hurt more for her to know Dad was confiding in another woman, rather than just being physical with one. I hit send and waited.

The only thing constant is change, right? It felt like a big shift was happening in my life. As much as I longed for things to be different, for us to be a normal family, I didn't want it to happen this way. I didn't want to be like the "normal" fifty percent, or whatever, of kids whose parents are divorced. I'd watched Hannah go through this. She was a better friend, a better person, before her parents got divorced. Back in those days, in elementary school, she actually listened when I talked. She wasn't always trying to prove her worth to the world.

The phone rang, interrupting my thoughts.

"May I speak to Lola?"

"This is she."

"Hi, Lola. This is Bethanie. I was just calling to check in with you about the cheerleading schedule. Are you ready for camp next week?"

Cheerleading camp. I'd barely remembered. Nor was I very interested in going. "Yeah, I'm ready."

"That's fantastic! And when we get back from camp, the summer practices will begin on Tuesdays and Thursdays from four to six. Will you need a ride for those? I can put your name on the carpool list."

"My mom should be able to drive me to those. I'm good, thanks."

"Great! I'm really excited about this year and I think we'll have a great time cheering together."

"Me too," I said.

"Well, I guess I'll let you go now."

"Okay. See you next week."

"Oh, and Lola, you and Hannah are welcome to come to my back-to-school party. It'll be at my house the Saturday night before school starts. Pass on the invite to her and bring a date if you want."

Bethanie was inviting *me* to her party! "Thank you, we'll definitely be there." I hung up, excitement welling inside me.

When school started I really was going to be part of the group. They would get to know me for me and stop seeing me as the quiet girl who tags along with Hannah. Maybe . . . if we really became friends . . . I could invite Ian into the group. Everyone would figure out he *isn't* a freak. I wondered if I should invite him to the party. Probably not since we decided dating was a bad idea. That reminded me, I still hadn't talked to Hannah.

I picked up the phone. She'd left three messages for me since Friday night. Obviously, she had talked to her mom and I had been avoiding her. But with such good news, I hoped I could distract her from the topic of Ian.

"Guess what we just got invited to?" I said when she answered the phone.

"WTF, Lola? I've called you like five times this weekend. Why didn't you call me back?"

Hannah's concern almost shocked me. "A lot happened this weekend. I've been busy."

"Just, please, tell me you were not on a date with Ian White the other night."

I paused for a moment. "We're friends. That's all." It wasn't a lie.

"This is our year, babe. You better not be screwing it up by dating freaks!" she laughed. "So what's the big news?"

"We're invited to Bethanie's party!"

Hannah let out a squeal from the other end of the line. "Yes! We're in! So what exactly did she say?"

"You and Hannah are welcome to come to my party and bring dates if you want to."

"Dates?"

"Yeah, you got anybody in mind?"

"Andy's been flirting with me on Facebook. Maybe we could double with him and Camden."

"Camden? As in quarterback football star Camden?"

"Yes, he and Andy are best friends."

"Isn't he kind of a jerk though?" I couldn't imagine going on a date with Camden Collins. There was just no way he would be into me. It didn't matter if I was a cheerleader or if I was actually really popular, he was way out of my league. Plus, he wasn't Ian.

"True, he does have a bit of a reputation for being a player but he's so freakin' hot. And so not a weirdo!"

"I don't know, Hannah. He's not going to want to go out with me."

"Have a little confidence, my friend. We've got to get you off freak island and back to the real world. I'll be back home in two weeks. We'll go for a makeover. And, you know, it wouldn't hurt if you tried the Special K diet for a few weeks."

"Did you really just tell me to go on a diet?"

"What? NO! That was totally a joke. You look great just like you are." She shuffled the phone around and shouted something to someone on her end. "Hey, my dad needs my help. Gotta go. Let's talk later."

"Bye," I mumbled as the other line clicked.

I checked my email and there was no response from Ian yet. I was on my way downstairs when a key turned the lock on the front door. Mom had gone to her follow-up appointment with Dr. Koman so I figured it was my dad stopping by while she was gone.

"Hey there," he said when he walked in. "What's going on today?"

"Just wasting away another summer day."

"Feel like going apartment hunting with me?"

My heart sank. "Apartments?"

"I can't exactly stay in that hotel forever."

"Wow."

"I'm sorry. I know this is hard for you." He put his arm around me.

"It's just all happening so fast and, after Friday night, I thought you'd just come back." I looked at him.

"Friday night didn't have anything to do with our separation. You mom was just having a panic attack. She tried to relax herself is all."

"Maybe she wouldn't have had a panic attack if you hadn't walked out on us."

"I didn't walk out. I was going to do this slowly. She asked me to leave right away."

"I don't want you to get divorced. I don't want our family torn apart again."

"Again?"

I paused, deciding if I should tell Dad about the life I'd seen. "Forget it. I tried to tell Mom already. She said I was crazy."

"What are you talking about?"

"I don't want you to think I'm crazy too. Dr. Koman's got his hands full as it is," I laughed nervously.

"Lola, what in the world?"

What did I have to lose? Dad was leaving us anyway. "Okay, fine." I walked over and sat on the couch. Dad followed. I launched into the whole story starting with passing out on the Metro in DC and ending with the soldier holding the gun to my head.

"Whoa," he said when I was done. "Past life? Really?"

"Yeah. Ian says it must relate to this life or I wouldn't be seeing it. You said that Zandria tried to get you to stay with us. Maybe it's karma for what she did in that life. What if you are supposed to stay this time because you have a choice?"

"I can't stay. I'm done." He leaned forward and rubbed his hands across his thighs. "And it sounds like you're just having some vivid dreams."

"No, Dad. It's real. Ian's mom does hypnosis and she's seen people go back to past lives. The Buddhist and Hindus believe in reincarnation. It's not crazy."

"I didn't say it was crazy. Just sounds like a dream is all."

"But Dad, remember how you felt in that room at the museum? Maybe that was because you were actually in one of those camps. Maybe it *was* familiar. And Mom was so in love with you that day. We felt that life when we were in the museum. I know we did." I paused, trying not to cry. "What if this time, you're supposed to stay? We couldn't stay a family then, but we can now."

Dad stood up and looked at me. "Lola, I've got an appointment to see an apartment in thirty minutes. Do you want to come with me or not?" He glimpsed at his watch then walked out the front door.

I didn't want to go with him, but I didn't want to stay there alone either. I dialed Mom's cell. We'd made an agreement that she'd have it charged and turned on at all times now. She answered.

"Hey, Mom. I just wanted to let you know I'm going out with Dad for a little bit. If I'm not here when you get home, don't worry."

I hung up and went to join Dad at his car.

We drove across town to an older neighborhood close to the historic district. Dad stopped in front of a white duplex. A little old man stood in the front yard and waved at us when we pulled up. Dad got out of the car, but I sat staring for a moment.

"You coming?" Dad leaned into the car before closing his door.

The man's name was Mr. Smith. He'd owned the duplex since 1960 when he bought it brand new. He lived in the left side and rented out the right side. He opened the door and stepped back so my dad and I could go in first. It was a cute space with hardwood floors and high ceilings. There were two bedrooms and a small sunroom off the back. Mr. Smith told us that had been a later addition.

"Which room do you like, missy?" Mr. Smith asked.

They were both small with tiny closets. I slid my foot across the hard floor and thought about how I'd miss the vacuum lines. "I like carpet."

"Think of the time you'll save by not having to vacuum," Dad laughed.

I looked at him. "I like vacuuming."

"I know." He put his arm around me. "Can you give us a minute, Mr. Smith?"

"Sure thing, Mr. Ray." Mr. Smith shuffled out of the room.

"This place is a great deal. What do you think? Could you handle calling this place home some of the time?"

I looked around the room and let out a deep sigh. "It's a cute little place."

"The neighborhood is nice and with Mr. Smith next door we'll never have to worry about rowdy neighbors."

I remembered Ian's story of the apartment complex Wayne lived in after his parents separated. At least I wouldn't have to live in a place like that. "It's really far from school, Dad."

"I work from home, though. I'll drive you in. It won't be a problem."

"What if you decide to come back home?"

"I'm not going to come back home." Dad took my hands and looked into my eyes. "I'm so sorry to do this, but I just have no choice anymore. Hopefully you'll never have to feel the way I feel, but if you do, you'll know. I can't force it anymore."

I leaned into him and buried my face in his shoulder. I realized how small he was, yet big enough to change the course of my life. "This place will be fine," I said with my head still on his shoulder.

Dad wrote the deposit check to Mr. Smith and took me out for ice cream. For him, it was a celebratory treat, for me it was comfort food. It felt like another nail in the coffin of my desires for a normal family life, with two parents happy and together. I wanted to run home and over to Ian's house. But Ian wasn't across the street this week, so all I could hope for was a reply to my email.

Chapter 20

Dad didn't come inside when he took me back home. He let me out in the driveway and waited until I opened the door to pull out. Mom joined me at the window as I watched him leave.

"So where did the betraying jerk take you anyway?" she asked looking over my shoulder.

"Mom, he didn't betray you."

"Some would argue an emotional affair is worse than an actual affair."

"Since when does a friendship count as an affair?" I looked at her.

"In my opinion, if she doesn't work with him, there's no reason to be friendly." She twisted her long hair up. "So where did he take you?"

"Apartment hunting."

She stopped in front of the couch and sat down. A look of worry washed over her face.

"You okay?" I sat down beside her.

She blinked hard and the fear in her eyes disappeared. "Yeah. Did he find a place?"

"A little duplex on Oak Street."

"Oak Street? That's not in the school district."

"It'll be fine. I'll be with you most of the time anyway." I reached for her hand.

She brought my hand to her lips and kissed it. It was her way of saying thank you. "Ian called a little bit ago."

"What time?" I asked.

"I don't know, a half hour ago. I'm not sure about that boy anymore."

I got up from the couch and ran to my room, ignoring what she'd said.

"Hey there!" I said when Ian answered the phone.

"Did you really send me an email?"

"So you got it then?"

"I got it. I just didn't realize we'd become friends who email. You know you can call me right?"

"I forgot your mom's number, that's all," I lied.

"That painting's pretty hardcore, huh? Crazy. Did it look exactly like the vision?"

"I mean I don't really know what I looked like in that life. Other than knowing I was skinny, I haven't seen my face and probably won't. But the woman was definitely Mom."

"Did your mom freak when you told her about the life?"

"She just didn't believe it. Period."

"Want my mom to talk to her?" Ian asked.

"Oh, gosh no. Talk about weird getting weirder."

"Why don't you slip the book I gave you into her room? Maybe she'll pick it up and start reading it without any nudging from you."

"Maybe."

"Is she going to be all right with everything?" Ian asked.

"I hope so. She's on new meds, so that's good. If nothing else, they'll keep her in an induced state of euphoria."

"Ah, yes. Ignorance is bliss," Ian laughed. "Leave it to man to come up with a drug that keeps you from feeling all the stuff you're supposed to feel."

"Mom's bipolar, Ian. That's different. She can't function without them."

"I'd say she does function, just not the way everyone thinks she's supposed to. They want us all to be consumerist robots."

"Oh, that's great, Ian. Why don't you try living with a crazy person and see how it feels. I've spent most of my life waiting for the ball to drop. Friday night, I was sure it finally had."

"I'm sorry. That was insensitive."

"At least your parents decided together to split up and you didn't have a crazy mom drive your dad away. Now I'm stuck taking care of her. I can barely even take care of myself. It really sucks."

I heard footsteps rush down the stairs. Panic rushed over me. I dropped the phone and ran to the door. Mom disappeared around the corner. She must have heard the whole conversation.

I picked the phone back up. "Lola? Hello? You there?"

"Crap, Mom was standing outside the door and she heard everything." I paced back and forth. "I gotta go."

I ran downstairs. When I got to her bedroom, the door was closed and locked. I knocked gently. "Can I come in?"

"Go away."

"Mom, I am so sorry. Please let me come in and talk to you."

"I'm feeling a bit irrational and crazy right now. I'd hate to expose you to that, so if you don't mind I'd prefer to be left alone."

"I didn't mean that the way it sounded. I love you." I pressed my forehead to the locked door.

There was no reply from the other side. Just silence. I shook the knob one more time. I never should have said that stuff to Ian. How could I have been that thoughtless and careless?

"I'm starting dinner now." I walked away from the door and

looked through the cabinets for something to fix for dinner.

Mom finally came out of her bedroom when dinner was on the table and slightly cold. I stayed seated at the table in front of my plate, even though I'd finished eating, waiting and hoping she'd join me.

She sat down quietly and scooped some cheesy tuna-mac onto her plate. "Thank you for dinner," she said, swallowing her first bite.

I could barely look her in the eyes, thinking of how much I'd hurt her. What I'd said was just horrible. Could she forgive me? "I'm really sorry. I shouldn't have said any of that." I looked down at my plate. "You take care of me more than I take care of you. I didn't mean for it to come out like that. I was just irritated at something Ian said."

"More importantly, you didn't expect me to hear it, which hurts me all the more. I don't like knowing you're talking about me instead of talking to me." She put down her fork and leaned back in the chair. "We have to be a team now. I need you to communicate with me. Things are going to be more different than they've ever been and we've got to adjust. If you have a problem with what I'm doing or not doing, I need to know."

"I know." I shifted my glass of water back and forth nervously. "I just want you to stay on the medicine."

"Assuming this medicine works the way Koman thinks it will, I can definitely do that."

"I love you." I smiled at her.

"I love you too." She wiped a tear that was welling up in her eye. I let out the breath I'd been holding.

The week passed and Mom seemed to be getting along fine. We had a family session with Dad and Dr. Koman where we talked openly about Dad's friendship with Zandria. Dad admitted to having a crush at first. He'd initially mistaken Zandria's friendliness for more, but soon realized it wasn't. Mom ranted and raved for a bit, but in the end, she understood the situation enough to move on. When I told Ian about the session, he suggested that maybe Zandria had come into our lives only to make peace with Dad. Her role had nothing to do with hurting or healing our family, but only to receive forgiveness for the pain she caused my father in the last life. Even if she couldn't actually apologize, their souls would understand what their friendship this time around meant. All they really needed was an adequate amount of love to counter the hate from the past. If they'd been more than friends in this present moment, it would have only added to the pain, rather than healing it. With that thought firmly planted in my mind, I could let go of hate towards her as well. For whatever reason, my family just wasn't meant to stay together this time either.

Ian arrived back at his Dad's on Saturday, just two days before I had to leave for cheerleading camp. We met in his driveway the night before I was leaving.

"It sucks that you're leaving tomorrow," he said as he skateboarded back and forth in the road.

"Do you mind giving that thing a break?" I asked, remembering getting caught by my dad the last time we'd met like this.

He flipped the board into the air and caught it. "Sorry, too loud, huh?"

"I'm pretty sure my mom would sleep through a hurricane, but she is weaning herself off the sleeping pills, so you never know."

"You ready for cheerleading camp?"

"I have no idea what I'm getting myself into, actually. I don't belong with those girls." I picked at my broken fingernail.

"Of course, you do. You're beautiful."

My stomach flipped. Ian thought I was beautiful. Me? "Um, have you seen Bethanie and Anna? Those girls look like models. I'm a potato head compared to them."

"You're too hard on yourself. You are as pretty and as cool as any of those girls. More so, if you want my opinion."

"You know, you're the best friend I've ever had." I looked at Ian, amazed at what I felt for him. He gave me butterflies, yet also made me feel perfectly at home. "I didn't say anything when you called me your best friend that night, but I feel the same way. I'm glad that nothing has changed. I was really worried after what happened."

"What are you talking about? Nothing happened. We're friends, have always been and will hopefully always be." He took off his baseball hat. His wavy dark hair fell onto his forehead covering his eyes.

"So, do you happen to know any story lines on the MTV reality shows?" I asked to break the silence.

"What?" Ian asked.

"I've forgotten to watch all summer. What if they ask me about it at camp?"

"Did you ever watch those shows?"

My face got hot.

"Oh, my gosh, you did." Ian leaned back shaking with laughter.

"I had to watch them with Hannah."

"Right, blame it on Hannah." Ian nudged me with his shoulder. "You're just lucky that I already love you."

I was stunned. Ian said he loved me. Why did he say it? Was he going to kiss me? What did this mean for our promise to just be friends? What would I tell Hannah? Oh, my God. "You what?" I finally asked.

"Love you. As a friend, you know."

My heart dropped. "Oh, yeah, of course. As a friend." I

pretended that I knew exactly what he meant. But I had hoped that he just loved me, period.

The next morning, Dad arrived at eight to take me to school to catch the bus to camp. When we pulled into the parking lot, most of the other girls were there.

"Well, here we are," Dad said.

"Yep."

"You haven't been away from home like this since that beach trip with Hannah's family two years ago. Are you nervous?"

"Only a little bit, but I'll be okay." I smiled at my dad. He squeezed my hand.

"I've been meaning to tell you and I guess now is as good a time as any."

A nervous feeling hit me. "Tell me what?" I asked.

"Tomorrow's moving day. I've got a couple of guys to help move my stuff. And your mom and I've already decided what I can take to my place." He searched my face for a reaction. "So when you get back, you'll have another place to call home."

I was stunned. "I wish you'd have told me sooner. I don't know what to say now."

Bethanie approached the car. "Hi, Lola. Can I help you load your stuff onto the bus?"

I looked at Dad and then back at Bethanie. "Sure," I replied and stepped out of the car. My shock turned to anger.

Dad climbed out and opened the trunk. Bethanie grabbed my tote and I took the sleeping bag and pillow.

"Let me take that." Dad reached for the pillow.

"No," I snatched it away. "I've got it. I don't need your help."

Bethanie and I walked side-by-side toward the charter bus. I looked back and saw Dad's pleading eyes. He wanted me to say it was okay, but it wasn't. I knew he was moving out for good, but why did he plan it without me?

I loaded my things on the bottom of the bus as intense dread built up inside me. It was the worst possible time to leave Mom. Dad was really going through with it. How was she going to handle this? I fought back the urge to cry. I had no choice but to get on the bus or I'd be kicked off the squad. How could he move while I was away? I looked over at him as he leaned on the hood of his car, waiting for me to say goodbye. I walked toward the door of the bus instead. I waved to him as I stepped on. He blew me a kiss. I smiled, but didn't return it.

From the window, I watched him. He stayed there, leaning on the car until the engine started and the bus pulled away. I guess I could consider this camp an escape from the upheaval of my fifteenth summer. As much as I didn't want to go, maybe I'd find a bit of that normal I longed for with these girls around me.

"E-A, E-A-G-L, E-A-G-L-E-S, Eagles! Woo, Woo!" Bethanie shouted the cheer as the bus entered the highway. The rest of the girls joined in. I did too, but the words stuck in my throat.

Chapter 21

Five days later, when we arrived in the school parking lot, Dad was waiting inside his car pressing buttons on his phone. His cell phone overuse didn't bug me the way it once had. There was no looming doom going through my head, wondering who he was communicating with, as he pressed on the small screen. The deal was done. He looked up from his phone and smiled as I approached the car. My anger toward him had subsided while I was gone. Being away gave me some time to clear my head, make peace. I still wished he'd included me in the official move. It felt almost like helping him move would have helped me somehow too.

"Hey, you surprised me," he said through the open window.

"You were pretty entranced by that thing," I replied.

"Yeah, sending out an email to a guy I just got a contract with," he smiled. "It's a big one. Could make or break me."

"Well, I hope it doesn't break you." I nodded and carried my bag toward the trunk. Dad got out of the car and followed me.

Once my things were loaded, we left the school lot. Bethanie shook her pom-poms at me as we passed.

"Looks like you made a new friend," Dad said.

"Maybe," I mumbled staring out the window. Dad turned left instead of right. "Where are you going?" I asked.

"I want you to see my place."

My heart sank. "I'm really tired. Can we do it another day?" I just wasn't ready to see Dad's new home. I still didn't want it to be real.

Disappointment clouded his eyes. "I guess so," he answered and pulled into a gas station to turn around.

We arrived at our house, or rather Mom's house, in less than ten minutes. Dad carried in the sleeping bag and pillow, while I grabbed the bag and my new pom-poms.

"There she is, my little cheerleader!" Mom grabbed the pom-poms out of my hand and clapped them together. "I always wanted to be a cheerleader, but you know me, just not peppy enough."

"You're peppy today." I put my bag down and hugged her.

"Well, look at the lovely couch your father bought me."

I allowed myself a moment to look around the room. It was definitely not the same as five days before though, other than the couch, most of the differences were subtle ones.

Dad put the sleeping bag and pillow down on the steps and walked to the couch. "Yep, we decided I could have the old one if your mother got a new one. Hence, we picked this one up yesterday."

I sat down in the middle of the new eggplant-colored couch and bounced a little. "It's nice."

The room was quiet for a bit and the air grew tense. "All right, I'm going to get out of here now," Dad said and leaned down to hug me. "Mom and I haven't come to an agreement just yet," he whispered in my ear, "but I hope you'll come stay at my place this weekend." He kissed me on the forehead before walking toward the door.

When the door closed behind him, Mom joined me on the couch. "You didn't go to see the new place?" she asked.

I shook my head. "Have you?"

"Lord no! Your dad doesn't want me in that place."

"But you went shopping together. You're getting along, right?"

"As well as any estranged husband and wife can, I suppose." She twisted at a strand of her long blonde hair.

"How does the office look?" I asked.

"Empty."

"What are we going to do with the space?"

"Take in a boarder," Mom laughed.

I pushed her playfully then rested my head on her shoulder. "Really, what are we going to do with it?"

"I wasn't completely joking about the boarder idea. I have considered it. I'm not sure how we'll get through this on our budget."

"Dad has to help pay for stuff."

"Yes, but even so, he has his own rent to pay now. Things are going to be tight." She sighed. "I'm going to have to get rid of the studio space."

"But you love that place." I sat up and looked at her.

"Life's choices aren't always easy."

"Well, we'll have to make the office into a home studio then," I smiled and took her hand.

"You look tired, baby. Why don't you go take a nap?"

"That actually sounds good." I got up from the new couch and carried my things upstairs.

I dropped the bag in my room and carried the sleeping bag and pillow into Dad's office. I wanted to sleep where Dad had for so long. In some weird way, I thought I might feel close to him. When I stepped in, I was taken aback by the bareness of it. I made myself a pallet on the floor and drifted off to sleep. Before I fell into dreamland, I made one request. *Show me what happens next.*

I am on the ground and the young man stands before me, pointing the gun at me. His hand trembles. I stare into his eyes and see tears welling up. Without saying a word, I plead with him to spare me. He doesn't look away, even though he should refuse to meet my gaze. My mother wails my name. I do not look at her. I hear a guard's fist hit her face. I don't want to see it. The sound is more than I can bear.

"Shoot her!" the older guard orders from his place at my mother's side.

The young one doesn't flinch. His hand is on the trigger, but he is frozen. His eyes stay fixed on mine. The way he stares, it's almost like he loves me. I know this is impossible and yet it feels true.

"Pull the trigger, idiot!" The angry one races toward us.

The young one doesn't move.

I close my eyes and lower my head to the ground. I recite a prayer, one I'd learned for my bat mitzvah. I am trying to be a strong woman, yet the sound of my mother shrieking causes me to sob like a baby. Then I hear the shot.

Pain courses through my side. Soon I am drenched in blood. I look at the young soldier. His gun is now at his side and he's staring, dumbstruck, at the older guard. He didn't pull the trigger. He couldn't.

"Now, traitor, you can watch her die a slow death." The old guard spits in the young one's face. The boy looks down at me.

Tomorrow is my birthday. I will be sixteen. But that's not what I want now. I want out of this body, away from this pain, out of this life. And I want out now. I reach out to the young Nazi, much like the little boy at the train station. "Have mercy on me," I beg.

He knows exactly what I'm asking. I watch him lift the gun, still trembling. Just before he pulls the trigger, a tear slips down his cheek.

I find myself high above, looking down on the scene. The young one falls to his knees and rocks back and forth. My mother breaks free of the line of women and runs to my side. She scoops me into her arms and wails at the loss of her only child.

My father is a mile away on the other side of the camp, in a barber chair trying to be strong and stay hopeful for his beloved daughter and wife.

"Lola, Lola, wake up!" Mom shook me awake.

I opened my eyes and met hers.

"You scared me," she said.

"I finally saw how it ended." My eyes were wet with tears, my body still shaking from the dream.

She rubbed a hand across my forehead. "It was a dream, Lola, just a bad dream."

I shook my head. "No, I don't think it's a dream. I've never had a dream so real. It's our last life together."

"If you don't stop talking like this, I'll have to take you to Dr. Koman."

"Before I fell asleep, I asked to see what was next. I've been seeing the end of that life little by little all summer."

"Lola." Mom seemed to surrender for a moment.

"The first time I saw it, we were on the train. That train was taking me to die. I don't know about you and Dad, but I was killed within an hour of being there. I just saw it, they shot me."

"Who shot you?"

"First, a young soldier was supposed to shoot me, but he couldn't. I think he loved me. Then . . ."

Mom put her hand up and shook her head. "That's enough.

It's a dream, it's all a dream." She got up and walked away.

I lay on the sleeping bag staring at the ceiling. Who was the young man? He had to be someone from this life. Did I know him yet or would he show up some time in the future?

As I lay there unraveling the dream, the phone rang.

"Lola," Mom called from the bottom of the steps. "Ian's calling."

I went into my room and grabbed the phone.

"Hello, my cheerleader friend. Did they brainwash you or is the Lola I know still in there?"

I smiled at the sound of his voice. "I am adequately schooled in fashion, cell phones, and TV shows, but other than that, I'm still here."

"Am I going to have to watch some stupid reality shows with you now?"

"Hey, I play video games with you."

"That doesn't count. You like them just as much as I do," Ian laughed. "So what else is new?"

"I saw the end."

"End to what?" Ian asked.

"The life in the Holocaust. I relived my own death."

"Whoa."

"I know, right?"

"Tell me about it."

"A young guard did it. At first, they ordered him to do it, but he couldn't. Then an older guard stepped forward and shot me in the side. He called the younger one a traitor and told him to watch me die slowly. That was when the young one killed me. Out of mercy, so I wouldn't suffer."

"I can't believe he didn't follow the orders."

"It sounds ridiculous, but I really felt like he loved me. I don't know why or how, but I looked into his eyes and I could see it."

"Wow."

"Yeah. And it was the day before my birthday. I was killed the day before I turned sixteen."

"What does that mean?"

"I have no idea, but like you said, if I need to figure it out, I suppose I will, in time."

"Do you know who the guy was?"

"That's another part I can't figure out."

"He doesn't look like anyone here?" Ian asked.

"Not that I recognized."

"Want to try to go back there? I can hypnotize you again."

"I don't really want to go back. Why does it matter so much anyway?"

"Well, it's just," Ian stammered, "I wanna know if I'm there. I can't stop thinking about it. Have you seen me? Could it be . . ." his voice trailed off.

"Don't even suggest that. There's no way."

"Can we try to find out?" Ian asked.

"I'll think about it." I felt a twinge of pain in my side. "But for the record, I just don't see how knowing who killed me will help me."

Chapter 22

The dream haunted me. Honestly, I was terrified to go back there. As Ian nagged me during the day to let him put me under, I prayed for protection from the dream each night before going to sleep. I couldn't stand the thought of experiencing my own death again and, even more than that, I didn't want to see my parents suffer without me. I'd seen them both when I rose out of that body. Was I supposed to see more or was that the end? And, of course, the mystery of the young man was still left unanswered. Maybe I wouldn't meet him until some future date. I was almost sixteen in the dream. In this life, I'd only been fifteen for over a month.

That weekend, I went to stay with Dad at my new home away from home. On Friday night, we ate dinner on trays in front of the television. We watched a show about a woman who had the power of dream. She was able to use the information she received in those dreams to solve crimes in the present. I felt a strange sort of affinity for this crime-solving heroine.

"I had another dream," I told Dad after the show ended.

He stood up and took our plates to the sink. I turned around on the couch and watched him.

"Dare I ask what happened?" he called over the running water.

"I experienced my own death."

He turned off the water and leaned against the counter. I walked over to the bar that separated the kitchen from the living room.

"I was shot right in front of Mom. And the guard who shot me seemed to have feelings for me."

Dad shook his head and turned back to the dishes.

That wasn't the reaction I wanted. I couldn't handle him reacting the way Mom did. I needed to talk about this with one of them. It seemed so important to us. I grabbed a towel and joined him at the sink. "Say something."

"I don't know what to say." He handed me a plate to dry. "After what you told me about Zandria, I got to thinking about my conversations with her. When she first introduced herself to me online, she said she felt intuitively drawn to me, like we had something to work out."

"Why didn't you tell me that before?"

"I never gave her ideas much thought. She believes in something she calls soul contracts. She thinks we're all fulfilling promises we made to each other before we were even born. I put as much stock into that idea as I do miracle sightings of Jesus or Mary."

"So, you think she's crazy?"

"No, I just thought the idea was wishful thinking. Giving meaning to what is little more than chaos."

"It is an interesting theory, though."

Dad laughed. "You'll have to share it with dream detective, Ian."

I went to bed that night thinking about soul contracts. The idea fit with everything Ian had told me, though he'd never called it that. I still wasn't ready to revisit the dream. I felt my heart start to race as I closed my eyes. I asked for protection before I drifted off to sleep.

On Monday morning, Hannah called to tell me she was back in town. She wanted to know if I was up for a trip to the pool. I agreed with the sad realization that my first trip to the pool would take place during the last two weeks of summer break.

"What time will you be here to get me?" I asked.

"Will your mom take us? My mom's at work."

"No problem. We'll come get you in an hour." I hung up and ran downstairs.

Mom sat at the table jotting in her lesson plan book. She'd report back to work next week, one week before the students. "You look chipper this morning. Who was that on the phone?"

"Hannah. She wants to go to the pool."

"So you're going back to the old sidekick then?"

"What's that supposed to mean? Nothing's changed. Hannah was just away for the summer." Actually everything had changed and I wasn't sure if my friendship with Hannah could still be normal.

"Well, don't get me wrong. I'm glad you're getting out in the sun instead of staying cooped up indoors playing video games, but isn't this the same girl who thinks your new best friend is a weirdo? How is that going to work exactly?"

"Ian's at Joan's this week and I really think I can be friends with both of them. Once Hannah gets to know him, she'll realize how cool he really is." I put a frozen waffle into the toaster. "Can you drive us to the pool?"

"Sure. I'll take you on my way to clean out the studio."

The toaster popped, I wrapped the waffle in a napkin and went back upstairs. I searched through my chest of drawers looking for the bathing suit we'd bought at the end of the summer last year. I found it at the bottom of the second drawer, a floral tank top with a black-skirted bottom. Mom had begged me to get the regular bikini bottoms. Last summer, I'd put on some extra weight and finally realized my hips and thighs were not the size of a child's anymore. I hated my pear-shaped figure, but Mom had boasted that I was lucky to have such extraordinary child-bearing hips. She wanted me to be proud of who I was, flaws and all. Instead, I chose the suit that would hide as much of me as possible.

I changed into the grandma bikini and stared in the mirror, confident that the worst of my body was covered. Mom's voice ran through my mind, reminding me to love myself just as I was. It was odd that a woman who was prone to falling into deep holes of self-loathing could be so persistent about teaching her child to express self-love. *Do as I say, not as I do.* Isn't that how the saying goes?

"Hey, Mimi," Mom remarked when I came down in my suit.

"Mimi?"

"Yep, that's what we called my grandma when I was a little girl." Mom laughed. "She had a bathing suit just like that."

I glared at her.

"I'm sorry, Lola! I just wish you weren't so modest. You have a beautiful body. I would kill for those curves."

Mom dropped Hannah and me off at the pool an hour later. Hannah scoped out the lounge chairs until she found the perfect spot. "There he is! Come on." She grabbed my elbow and pulled me along.

"There who is?" I caught a glimpse of Andy at the same time I asked the question.

"Andy!" Hannah waved like the pageant girl she was.

I looked around the pool, praying Camden wasn't with him. I didn't really even want to be around him, let alone have him see me in a bathing suit. Just then, we heard a voice from behind.

"Hey, ladies?"

I turned around. It was Camden.

"Hey, Cam," Hannah said.

"Cam-den actually," he corrected her.

"Why didn't you tell me they were going to be here?" I whispered into Hannah's ear.

"Would you have come if you knew?"

I shook my head and followed her and Camden to the lounge chairs Andy had saved for us.

Andy stood up and gave Hannah a big hug. "I'm glad you got a ride to the pool."

I should have known this was more than just Hannah wanting to catch up with her best friend. "Andy, you know my friend Lola, right?"

"I think I've seen you around. You made the varsity cheerleading squad, right?"

I nodded and smiled, wishing I was someplace else.

"I'm headed in to cool off." Andy pointed toward the water. "Want to come?"

Hannah took his hand and both of them looked at me. "I'm going to sit here for a few minutes first," I replied.

Camden sat in the lounge chair next to Andy's. He was playing with his phone while wearing ear buds and nodding slightly in rhythm. It was as good a sign as any that he didn't want to get to know me better. I spread my towel out on the chair beside the one Hannah had dropped her bag on. I searched through my bag, wishing I'd thrown in a book or at least my iPod. I leaned the chair back and inconspicuously pulled the t-shirt I was wearing over my head. I placed it over my face, in part to keep the sun out, but also to demonstrate to Camden I was equally disinterested in him.

When Hannah and Andy returned from their brief dip in the

pool, Hannah laughed loudly. I pulled the t-shirt off my eyes just in time to see Andy holding a kid's bucket and pouring water on Camden, who had put down his phone and was listening to music with his eyes closed.

"Dude, what the hell? You better not have gotten my phone wet, you little snot!" Camden jumped up and went after Andy who quickly did a cannonball back into the pool. Camden just shook his head and went back to the lounge chair.

"I'm gonna kick his ass," he mumbled.

Hannah leaned over toward me. "Andy's so funny, don't you think?"

I looked at the ladder where Andy emerged from the water, shaking his head around like a dog climbing out of a bath. "I guess so."

"You guess so? That's it?"

"He's funny, Hannah, okay?"

Andy walked up and stood in front of Hannah's chair. "You want something to drink?"

"Sure," she smiled.

"All right, be back in a few." He turned toward the snack bar.

"What's wrong with you? You're really bitchy today. Actually, you've been bitchy all summer."

"It's been a hard summer with my parents."

"So what, Lola. Parents fight. It's life."

I sat up in the chair and glared at her. "You don't pay attention to anything that doesn't affect you. My dad moved out. My parents are getting divorced."

"I'm sorry. I, uh, guess I didn't know it was that serious," she stammered.

"You would have if you'd been interested in something besides who I'm hanging out with and how it might hurt your reputation."

Andy came back and passed Hannah a can of soda.

"Thank you." She pulled the empty lounge chair closer to hers and patted the seat. Andy sat down in it. I went to dip my feet in the water.

As I sat on the edge, I looked around the pool. Toddlers in swim diapers were splashing in the baby area while their mothers stood to the side chatting. A group of tween girls were gathered in the corner of the shallow end giggling and pointing at the male lifeguard. The lifeguard watched carefully as a boy about Sammy's age jumped in and out of the pool. The sky was blue, the sun was shining brightly, and the temperature was surprisingly cool for August. Usually, it was sweltering this time of year, but today it was simply hot. I looked over my shoulder at my friends, if I dared to call them that. Andy was whispering in Hannah's ear. She laughed and leaned into him, looking incredibly happy. Camden gawked at a thin college girl in a string bikini. *This* was the normal life I'd longed for, but all I wanted to do was go home and hang out with Ian.

I tried to imagine what he might look like here at the pool in a bathing suit. He was so thin and his skin so light, but still, I bet he'd be cute. I wondered what his bare chest looked like. For a guy, he was as modest as I was. The few times I'd glimpsed him mowing the lawn, he did it with his shirt on. It didn't matter to me, though. I'd gotten to where I didn't notice his flaws at all. To me, Ian was more attractive than Camden, with his blue eyes, sandy blonde hair, and bulging biceps. When I looked at Camden, the lyrics to that Carly Simon song my mom used to sing drifted through my head. *You're so vain, you probably think this song is about you.*

I walked to the snack bar to find out the time. I was stuck there for a few more hours, trying to ignore Hannah and Andy's displays of public affection while avoiding Camden as much as he was avoiding me.

Chapter 23

Mom arrived at the pool to get Hannah and me a half hour after the guys left.

"Mrs. Ray, I'm really sorry to hear about your separation." Hannah leaned forward from the back seat as we pulled into her neighborhood. The pageant world and growing up an only child had certainly given Hannah the confidence to talk to adults like she was one.

Mom reached over and patted her hand. "Thank you, sweetie."

"If you ever need to talk to anyone about divorce, you can call my mom." We pulled into the driveway in front of the large brick house Hannah had grown up in. "See ya later, Lola. Call me." She climbed out of the car.

"Bye," I yelled through the open window as she walked into the garage.

"Did you two have fun?" Mom asked.

"We met her new boyfriend and the jerk quarterback there, so I'd hardly call it fun."

"So you didn't hit it off with the quarterback?

I laughed. "Are you kidding?"

"Hey, you and Ian are just friends right?"

"Yeah, but Camden? I'd have a better chance at getting a modeling contract than getting asked out by him." I shook my head and stared out the window. "He's not my type anyway."

"Well, at least you got your Vitamin D," Mom laughed.

"Ah, yes. A bright side."

When we got home, I called Ian. "Save me," I moaned when he answered.

"What do you need to be saved from?"

"I just spent half the day with Hannah, Andy, and Camden at the pool."

"OMG! Those guys are totally super cool. I mean, they are gorgeous with a capitol G!" Ian was doing his best shallow, ditzy girl impersonation. I could just imagine his head whipping back and forth.

I laughed. "I can't begin to tell you. It was a see-saw between great levels of embarrassment and intense boredom."

"How in the world could you possibly be embarrassed or bored by the super-jocks?"

"Well, let's see, Hannah and Andy were all over each other and the only words that came out of Camden's mouth all morning were a few insults directed at Andy." I grabbed a clean shirt out of my drawer and pulled it over my head. "Quite frankly, I think I'd rather experience my death in the Holocaust again than have to repeat this day."

"Perfect, when do you want to schedule an appointment?" Ian asked.

"Huh?"

"An appointment with your hypnotherapist."

"Oh," I laughed. "I was only kidding, you know."

"You need to go back one more time. You need to see the rest, to know what happens to your mom and dad and the young guard." Ian paused. "Hell, maybe one more trip there and you'll figure out who he is."

"I don't know." The idea of seeing more of that life really scared me, but I felt like I should consider doing it for Ian. He'd helped me so much with all of this. If not for him guiding me through it, I might be penciled in on Dr. Koman's schedule with Mom.

Ian's voice pleaded, "I'll keep you safe, Lola."

"You don't understand, though. It was so scary being there. I'm just not sure I can handle it."

"I know it was hard. I saw you that day at my house. But sometimes when something is this frightening, it means that you have to face it." He paused. "I just think you need to do this."

The young soldier's face flashed through my mind. Maybe it would help to figure out who he was. And I'd like to see what happened to Mom and Dad. Maybe it would explain what they're going through now. "Okay, I'll do it." I walked to the closet and grabbed the vacuum. "When and where?"

"I'll meet you at my dad's in the morning. Sammy's at art camp this week."

I hung up the phone and plugged in the vacuum. I pushed the machine back and forth, back and forth.

When I was finished vacuuming, I went downstairs to join Mom. She was making lasagna for dinner. When she pushed the dish into the oven she asked me to help her bring in the art supplies from her car. We carried in four boxes and a few clean canvases and took them up to Dad's old office.

"When does Ian get back from his mom's?" Mom asked.

"He's there all week, but he's coming over to his dad's tomorrow to hang out with me."

"Do you think he'd let us use his truck? There are a few things that won't fit into the Escape." Mom lifted up her hair and fanned the back of her neck. She looked exhausted.

"What else do you need to pick up?" I asked.

"Two tables, a collage, and my paintings."

"What if Ian and I go pick that stuff up tomorrow? Would that help you?"

Her face brightened. "Can you? That would be amazing!"

I put my arm around her. "Of course, we can."

The next morning, Ian called from across the street. I made some toast to take with me and grabbed the key to Mom's studio.

"You ready to get started?" He ushered me into the living room.

"Actually, I have a little bit of a detour for us this morning." I noticed he'd put a blanket in the recliner and plugged the CD player in. "Mom needs some help moving out of her studio space at the art park. I sort of volunteered us to go over there and get the tables and her paintings."

Ian eyed the room. I sensed that he was disappointed. "I guess we can do this later then."

"Thank you." I threw my arms around him for a quick hug. "You should have seen her last night. She was so tired and sad. The studio means the world to her and now she has to let it go. I just don't want anything to make the depression come back."

"I understand." He grabbed his keys off the counter and I followed him to the door.

We walked into the studio. The built-in shelves were empty and the supplies that had been strewn across the large table last time I was there were gone. The brightly painted canvases were leaning in a stack against the wall and the collage was sitting on top of the smaller table. Ian walked over and stared down at it as I flipped through the paintings.

"There's some powerful imagery in this thing," he remarked.

"Like what?"

"Well, you got this woman here, arms outstretched, a sort of desperate surrender in her eyes. Then there's this barren tree and cocoon. A lot of images of death and rebirth here is all. When did she do this?"

I walked over and stood beside Ian. "She started this one on my birthday and finished it last week."

I looked at all the images on the collage. With Ian's explanation, I was looking at it with new eyes. Had my Mom consciously chosen these pictures or had they chosen her? "What do you think it means?"

"That she's going to be okay."

"I hope you're right." Ian was standing so close that our arms touched a little. Neither of us moved. I wondered if he'd felt it, the electricity that passed from his skin to mine. I certainly did.

"I am." He patted my back. "Hey, is the painting you told me about here?"

I felt a twinge of disappointment when he walked over to the stack of paintings. "Yeah, it's in the stack." I followed him and pulled out the one of my mom and me in our last life together.

"That's incredible." Ian stared at the painting. "I've got an idea. What if I hypnotize you right here. We can use the painting as a prop to take you back there. It seems like, if you look at the image, it will pin-point the place in time you want to arrive. Maybe it will keep you from having to die again."

"Do you think that will work?"

"I have no idea, but it's worth a try." Ian looked at me, excitement in his eyes.

I started to feel anxious. But I didn't want to let him down. "Where do you want me to sit?" I asked.

Ian surveyed the room. "Sit over there against the wall. I'll hold the painting up in front of you."

"What about the music?"

"Lola, I'm not even sure you need me at all. As many times as you've gone back there, I almost think all it would take is closing your eyes and asking to see."

I sat down cross-legged and leaned back against the wall. Ian sat in front of me holding the painting. I studied the picture and reminded myself it was my mother and me. Ian started quoting from the script he'd read the first time we did this. Fear rose up within me and he reminded me that I was loved, protected and safe. He asked me to look at the picture and remember what it was like to be there. He counted backwards and my eyelids grew heavy.

I float above the scene. Looking down, I see my mother holding my body. Two guards approach her and pull her away from what's left of me. She kicks and screams for a second before falling limp in their arms. Her eyes are glazed over, the life drained from them. She is back in line with the other women and children. A few guards go through the line inspecting each woman and taking notes of any skills they mention. My mother is a wonderful seamstress. She worked in our shop sewing men's suits. She was one of the best. When the guard asks her about her skills, she doesn't say a word. He moves her to the line on the left. In front of her is a small elderly woman cradling an infant and behind her is a woman so thin you can see her ribs. The woman appears to be delirious with fever, carrying on a conversation with someone no one else can see. I know what this means. My mother is among the sick and weak. When the intake is complete, the guards lead the healthy women toward buildings that resemble dormitories. The sick, old and too young move slowly to the building with smoke rising from it. We'd heard rumors of the crematoriums. Before entering that dreaded place, the women are marched into another building and prepared for their death. I watch as a barber shaves my mother's flowing black hair and a dentist checks her teeth for fillings. I can't bear to see the rest.

I think of my father and in seconds I am there looking down on him. His head is shaved and he's wearing a uniform. They're tattooing him. He stares at the numbers on his arm, hope still lighting his eyes. He doesn't know that I am dead and that his beloved wife will join me within minutes. He's praying to make it through, that someone, the Russians maybe, will intervene and save us all. He's wondering if our house will still be standing when we arrive there again. His imagination is not wild or dark enough to envision the reality of this situation.

Time passes in a blink. I am still with my father, watching. I know my mother is gone, though I haven't met her here on this side of the veil. Isn't death the place to be reunited again? I look down on my father and he is crammed into a hard wooden bunk with nine other men. He is emaciated. I barely recognize him. He resembles a skeleton covered only in a thin layer of skin. The hope is gone from his eyes. He will die in that bed, under those men who've stolen the bread he'd saved for just this moment. In the morning, when everyone but my father arrives for work, the guards will find him. They will carry him to the trenches and throw his remains into the mass grave that is the reality of this place where Work is Freedom.

Ian rested his hand gently on my knee. I wasn't shaking, but my face was wet with tears.

"Are you okay?" he whispered.

I wiped the tears from my eyes and nodded.

"Do you want to talk about it?"

"We all died there. Mom was killed right after me. Dad, he endured months of suffering, until he just withered away."

Ian moved closer and put his arm around me. "I'm so sorry."

"What am I supposed to do with this information? Why did I see it?"

"Only you can know that," Ian answered.

"How will I know?"

"Ask for guidance?"

"Who am I supposed to ask?" I looked into his eyes.

Ian pulled his arm back and his eyes shifted from mine. "Well, truth be told, sometimes when I'm alone I like to confer with the Captain."

"The Captain?"

"Yeah, you know, the Captain." He pointed toward the sky.

"Are you telling me that my non-conformist friend, Ian White, believes in God?" I leaned against the wall, pondering the idea. "I mean, I thought at the very least you were agnostic."

He laughed. "I mean, I suppose we don't know anything for sure, but I do like to believe that *the Captain* is, in fact, real." He paused for a moment with a peaceful smile on his face. "When I ask for help with something, I usually get it."

"Give me an example."

He looked at me puzzled.

"I'm a skeptic. I want proof," I smiled.

Ian laughed again. "All right. Let's see." He thought for a minute. "Well, when Wayne moved us into the new house, I asked the Captain to make it bearable."

"And?"

"I walked into my new living room and found the cute girl across the street blowing out a birthday candle."

I blushed. "That was embarrassing." I hid my face with my hands.

"It was the best answer I've ever gotten to one of my requests."

I looked at him. His eyes were lit up. He was sharing a deep secret with me, giving me a gift. I loved it. I loved his honesty, his vulnerability. "So basically, you're telling me to pray for the answer."

"Pray? Gosh, no! Prayer is for desperate people. I'm telling you to ask to be given understanding of the situation. What do you need to learn about this life from that one?" Ian stood and began to fold up Mom's table. "It doesn't matter what or who you believe in, you just have to have faith the answers you need will come."

"And they will?"

"I think so." He pushed the last leg of the table and lifted it up. "Now you want to get that door for me?"

Chapter 24

When Ian and I got back home with the rest of the things from Mom's studio, we found her in the office, rolling green paint on the walls.

"Wow, Ms. Ray. It looks awesome." Ian placed the table on the floor in the middle of the room. "Do you need a hand?"

"That would be great!" Mom pointed to the roller in the corner.

"Looks like there's only one extra roller. I'll just make myself comfortable here." I sat down on the carpet in the doorway.

"Don't get too comfortable there. The trim on those walls needs to be taped up." She tossed me a roll of blue painter's tape.

After we finished painting, Mom served us sandwiches and turtle brownies she'd baked the day before.

"I'm proud of you, Mom." I squeezed her hand after she placed the tray of treats on the table.

"Why? Because I'm serving you instead of vice versa?"

"No, because you're choosing to be happy." I broke off a bite of brownie and dropped it in my mouth.

"Well, I always thought that your father was the backbone of this family and that without him we'd crumble, but I'm learning that isn't the case." She poured two glasses of milk and passed them to Ian and me. "The worst happened. Your dad left and we're still here and doing fine. Of course, I'm happy."

The worst happened. I held those words in my mind. Was Dad leaving really the worst that could happen to us? The visions I'd seen throughout the summer had proven a lot worse could happen to my family. Even though our cozy American dream life was becoming a lot less cozy, we were still alive and well. I'd wanted to convince Mom and Dad to believe in me and the visions I was having. I wanted them to understand we'd been a family before and faced tragedy. But why? Mom was feeling all right, strong even. Ian was constantly telling me that I would only see what I was strong enough to handle and what I needed to know. Mom didn't need to know her family had suffered a tragic ending the last time they were together. She didn't need to feel the pain of having her husband ripped away from her embrace or holding a lifeless child in her arms. She would never be strong enough to bear those memories. The Captain of her soul was protecting her. She thought my visions were crazy because there was nothing in them that could help her. Her strength could only be drawn from this moment, right now. Despite all that she had been through once upon a time, she was here now, prevailing over fear, pain, and depression. She was taking a stand for the life she had left.

After lunch and after the paint dried, Ian and I helped Mom put together her new studio.

"It looks great!" Mom untied the bandana from around her hair and the blonde strands fell against her face. Despite the specks of green paint on her cheeks, she looked radiant.

"Granted, I only saw the other studio half-empty, but I'd say this space is even better," Ian said.

"And it won't require any gas in the car to get here either," I added.

Mom sat down on the stool behind her work table. "Things always work out in the end, don't they?"

Dad decided to join Mom and me for dinner on Friday night when he came to pick me up. Mom made lasagna again. She had almost perfected the recipe.

"I hate you moved out of the studio, Christine." Dad set the table, while Mom sliced the lasagna. "All you had to do was talk to me. The new contract is going well. I could have paid the rent over there."

"Thank you, but I want to do it on my own. Plus, it would be a shame to waste that space up there."

"It could have been a guest room," Dad replied.

"For who, my sister? I doubt she'll visit anytime soon and she's the last family we've got."

"That's not true, Mom. We've got each other." I sat down and dished out a serving of salad.

Mom and Dad joined me at the table. "She's right, you know." Dad looked at me first, then Mom. "You and I will be connected forever and even though I may not live under the same roof anymore, I'm always here for you guys."

Mom smiled and blinked back a tear.

Dad noticed the emotion welling up and quickly changed the subject. "So, Lola, anymore trips back to the concentration camp?"

"Oh, good grief, Nick. Don't encourage that nonsense."

"I don't necessarily think it's nonsense," he replied.

"You have got to be kidding me. Everyone knows that's just a bunch of Eastern hullabaloo."

"You hear that, Lola? Everyone knows, so of course, it's settled."

And just like that, we were back. My messed up family was still alive and well, just slightly altered.

"You know, I think Mom is right. It was all just a recurring dream and I don't think I'll be going back there again."

Mom went back to start her teacher workdays on Monday and I went over to Ian's.

"So you want to try the hypnosis one more time?" He retrieved the video game from the console and selected another one for us to play.

"No, I don't think so."

"But we didn't even figure out who the young guard was. Don't you want to know?"

"Not really." I pressed the buttons on my controller to start the game.

"But what if he did love you?"

"If I'm meant to see it, it will come to me in its own way and time, right?"

"I suppose."

"Plus, he was the one who killed me."

"Out of mercy."

"Still." I looked at Ian. He stopped arguing.

That night, I stared at the wall and thought about the young soldier. I imagined the look in his eyes. Was he just a kind soul or could it have been love that kept him from following his orders?

This room is strange and unfamiliar. The walls are bare except for a Nazi flag that hangs in front of the bed. I'm not sure why I'm here, but grief, guilt, and sadness sweep over me. Then I see him, the young soldier who killed me. He sits on the end of the bed and stares at the flag. It is his emotions I feel. My new form,

outside of my body, seems to come with a great awareness. I know his thoughts, I feel his pain. He looks down at the blood flowing from a fresh wound on his arm. He's carved something into his skin. In his hand, he holds a gun. I was the first one he killed, or was ordered to kill. He's watched the men around him turn cold. They kill and recover. Soon, it becomes a game. He doesn't want to turn to stone. Recover. He wants to die with this strange love and guilt wrapped up in his heart. He imagines my face.

"I'm so sorry." He lifts the gun to his head. Boom.

I woke up with a start and the answer came to me. The young guard was Ian.

Chapter 25

"Andy will be here any minute. You ready?" Hannah's voice blared through the phone.

"I'm ready." I stood in front of the mirror, hardly recognizing myself in the mini skirt and high heels. What was I thinking, wearing heels? Mom insisted on buying them for me, but I was convinced it looked like I was trying too hard. They're going to think I'm an idiot.

"You better look hot, Lola. Remember this party—"

"Is very important. I know."

Twenty minutes later, a horn blared from the driveway. "They're not even going to come to the door?" Mom asked as I grabbed my keys.

"Apparently not." I leaned down and kissed her. "See you around midnight. Thanks for letting me stay out later tonight."

"Have fun."

When I got out to the driveway, Ian was leaning on the bed of his truck, holding his skateboard, and watching the car. I'd been avoiding him for a few days, hiding out at my dad's. After seeing that he was the young guard who killed me, I hadn't been able to face him. I wasn't sure what I'd say if he asked about it.

"Lola, hey," he called.

I paused and looked at the car. Hannah glared at me through the window. I looked back at Ian. "Hey." I reached for the car door.

"When will you be home? Want to meet tonight?"

I shook my head and climbed in the back seat. Learning the truth had changed things. On top of not wanting to face his questions, I also worried that I'd feel afraid of him. I know it was irrational, but if he killed me once, even out of mercy, maybe it could happen again.

"Holy crap! Is that that freak, Ian White?" Andy adjusted the rearview mirror to get a better look.

"Yeah, that's Ian," Hannah replied.

"Dude, Camden, reach under the seat and grab that can, bro."

Camden leaned down and pulled an empty soda can out from below the seat. Andy rolled down the passenger window. He backed the car slowly out of the driveway and stopped right in front of Ian and his truck.

"Chuck it, dude," he said to Camden.

Camden hurled the can out of the window. "Loser!" The can hit Ian right in the chest. Andy pressed hard on the accelerator and the tires screeched as we pulled away. I turned to see Ian standing in the middle of the road with his middle finger high in the air. I couldn't leave him there.

"Stop the car!" I called from the back seat.

"What?" Hannah looked at me, horrified, as the car screeched to a halt.

I looked at her. "I can't do this." I opened the door and climbed out. The car pulled away, tires spinning one more time.

I took off the heels and carried them the rest of the way back to Ian's driveway. He cursed under his breath as he stomped on the can. "Don't let those jerks get to you," I said.

He jumped, startled.

"Sorry, didn't mean to scare you," I smiled, my heart pounding in my chest.

"What are you doing here? I thought you were going to the party." He stepped closer to me, searching my face. Could he see all that I was feeling? It was certainly a rush of emotions, fear being the strongest. I was afraid of what I'd seen in the past and what this moment meant for my future.

I pushed through the fear. "I'd rather be here with you," I said and reached my hand out to him. He took it.

"Want to go watch some *Battlestar Gallactica*?"

I scrunched up my face.

"Or I could hypnotize you one last time. Find out who the killer was."

The boom sounded in my head. I looked down at Ian's hand in mine. I couldn't tell him the truth about my executioner. It would crush him. In that moment, the only thing that Ian had in common with that young guard was that he loved me. That was where I put my thoughts.

"Watching *Battlestar Gallactica* doesn't sound so bad after all."

He nodded and pulled me in for a hug.

An Unrequited Fall

The Past Lives of Lola Ray Book Two

Abby holds one end of the damp cotton sheet. I hold the other and we lift it over the clothesline. Papa hates it when I help Abby but I don't care, I love her. I stare at her face, the way her dark brown skin glistens in the heat. When I was little I used to turn her hands over and over in mine, fascinated by the contrast in the color of her skin. When I'd run my tiny fingers over her palms she'd whisper, "See, we not so different after all." Yes, I love Abby.

A horse whinnies in the distance, but it's the footsteps of my little cousin racing up the drive that really catches my attention.

"Lyla, Lyla, the new spooks are here!" Hanna yells with excitement in her voice.

I glance in Abby's direction. Her eyes dart toward the ground. "I don't want to hear you call them that again, Hanna."

"That's what my daddy calls them."

"Well, he's wrong."

"If he's so wrong, how come your daddy put him in charge of the slaves?"

I don't answer her question. The truth is Uncle Al is the meanest man in Georgia and since no one else in this county wants anything to do with my mother's brother, Papa made him overseer. Even his own wife ran away from him, which is the other reason he and Hanna live on Papa's plantation with us.

The horse drawn wagon comes into view. Uncle Al tips his hat to Hanna and me. In the back there are three new slaves, a woman, a man, and a boy about my age. I am struck by the sight of the boy. He doesn't look like any negro I've ever seen. He has light brown skin, green eyes, and hair as soft as silk. He might be the most beautiful thing I've ever seen.

"Miss Lyla!" Abby calls.

I reach over and take the other end of the quilt. When my eyes meet hers she shakes her head as if she can read my mind. Don't you even think about that boy, Lyla.

Look for
An Unrequited Fall, The Past Lives of Lola Ray Book Two,
coming in the fall of 2014.